Famous Amos
THE POWER IN YOU

Aloha Michael,

"Claim your Power!"

Wally Amos

7/30/89

10

SECRET
INGREDIENTS
FOR
INNER
STRENGTH

Famous Amos
THE
POWER
IN YOU

by
**Wally Amos
and Gregory Amos**

DONALD I. FINE, INC.
NEW YORK

Library of Congress Catalogue Card Number: 88-45365

ISBN: 1-55611-093-6

Manufactured in the United States of America

10 9 8 7 6 5 4 3 2 1

DESIGN: Stanley S. Drate/Folio Graphics Co. Inc.

*This book is dedicated with love
to my wife Christine,
who through our marriage
has helped me discover
the Power In Me.*

ACKNOWLEDGMENTS

I would like to thank God as the source of my life and everything in it.

I give thanks to and for all my family and friends and to any who feel they do not fit into either category.

I give thanks to my guru/daughter, Sarah, who has taught me more about life in four years than I learned in forty-seven.

I thank Gregory for putting words in my mouth.

I thank God again for helping me finish this book.

CONTENTS

INTRODUCTION

Aloha,

I have spent over fifty years of research in the laboratory of life. In the process, I have discovered that many of us have no idea just how powerful we actually are. We are totally unaware of the tremendous reservoir of inner strength we possess. We view others as powerful because of their position, money or title. Many of us live the majority of our days as victims of the infamous, though mysterious, "they." In looking at those external examples of power we lose sight of the real power—the inner power of every human being.

I wrote this book to share with you some of the ingredients that have helped me to better understand and express my power. My hope is that they'll help you reclaim your power, so that you may live your life in the joyful, harmonious, abundant style in which God intended.

I could give you my thoughts on the power we all have in us, but Russell Kemp summed it up quite well in a poem, "Claim Your Power."

"Claim your power! Start it flowing. Activate it in your mind. There's one mind and I'm it's power. Calmly say this, and you'll find you're the master, not a puppet. You are God's image, not a slave! You can triumph over trouble. There's power within you to save. Ever loving, ever waiting. Power in you heeds your word. You were born to be the victor, and to give up is absurd. Dare to listen! Dare to breathe deep! Now relax, and think with power. Claim your power. Claim your power. God is waiting! Claim your power."

You are the original power tool.

You do have the power to change your life and in so doing you will have positively changed the chemistry of the entire universe.

Claim your power today!

Thank you for choosing this book and from this xiii day forward, may you begin to express your inner power in all areas of your life.

WALLY AMOS

Famous Amos

The
Power
in You

1

THE POWER IN LOVE

Whatever the Question, Love Is the Answer

Early in my cookie career, I decided that no matter how rich or famous I became, or how many friends I had, my standard for measuring success would always come from love. Love is the most important thing in my life. It is truly the inner core of my being.

> Love is the strongest force in the universe.

I have come to realize that the power of love—which is so infinite, so great, so magnificent—was

2

indeed the key that unlocked my dreams. Love can also be your key to life's secrets. Just let it generate and flow out of you.

Think of love as the center of a wheel, with components such as attitude, self-esteem, commitment, integrity, giving, imagination, enthusiasm and faith all jutting out as the spokes of the wheel. Each of these ingredients has a power of its own, but in addition to that, the power of love is focused through them. By living my life in tune with these principles, I have achieved inner peace and the goals of my dreams.

Since I am really no different from you, you too can achieve inner peace and reach the goals of your dreams. I will even share with you some things I've learned on the way. The important thing to remember is that love is a force that is generated inside each and every one of us. Since it's there, you might as well use it.

Just what is love to YOU? Is it an intimate feeling you have for someone you're involved with? Is it a feeling you have about a material object? I saw a card that had a character on the outside with the words, "I fell in love." The inside of the card read, "Did you get any on you?" That's the usual kind of love we deal with—the man-woman type of love (more like boy-girl actually)—and it could be

termed falling in and out of LIKE. That type of love   3
also centers around sensual desire and that's not at
all what I'm talking about.

The love I mean is more than anything you've
ever dreamed or thought possible. It encompasses all
of life and is not segmented in any way. It is love
deeply rooted in spirituality, with GOD as its source.
When you are at peace with yourself and the world,
you can experience love for yourself and whomever
or whatever is in your world. When your life, heart
and mind are in turmoil, love is still there, but the
static you create is so great that you can't *experience*
love's gifts. Love is there be it an intimate relationship or in a job you're crazy about. You don't simply
love yourself, your family, your spouse or your work,
but rather, you love everything and everything is
love.

> Love does not discriminate against race, color,
> sex, creed, religion, height or weight.

Many times, we fail to see love in another
person because we are so busy judging that person.
Love from the heart enables you to separate people
and see them as God's children, which is love.
When you can do that you will never feel mistreated

4

or victimized. You can recognize the good and the love in a person no matter WHAT they do. When you do THAT, your love will be accepted, then returned.

When I started allowing love to express itself through my daily actions, my life ceased to be a struggle. Love became the magnet that attracted the very best of everything: positive relationships, a terrific outlook on life and the attainment of my goals.

The Love Triangles

In order to attain the level of love consciousness I'm talking about, you must consistently apply love to everything you think, do and say. If you're anything like I am you'll have a real problem remembering to do that. Also, if you're anything like I am, you'll need some kind of model to help you remember. So, I'll give you one that was given to me by a very dear friend, Abdul Aziz Said.

Take a blank piece of paper and draw a triangle on the top half. At the top of the triangle, write "love." At the bottom left point of the triangle, write "lover." At the bottom right point of the triangle, write "beloved." This is the inner triangle.

Now, on the bottom half of the paper, draw a

second triangle. At the top of the triangle, write "thought." At the bottom left point of the triangle, write "action." At the bottom right point of the triangle, write "word." This is the outer triangle.

Now your goal in life is to superimpose the two triangles. You begin to accomplish this by LETTING YOUR EVERY THOUGHT BE A THOUGHT OF LOVE. It does not matter if it is a thought of a rock, a tree, an insect or a person; it must always be a loving thought.

Your every action needs to be that of a *lover*. When you are a lover you do everything possible to please. You will go to any length to satisfy the one you pursue. So in your daily affairs all your actions must have those characteristics of a lover.

One who is *beloved* is one who is held in great affection. Your every word must be as one who is beloved. Your words must leave your mouth ever so gently and land with the weight of a feather. Choose words of nourishment, support, encouragement and praise. Visualize everyone you speak to as your beloved and let your words reflect it.

When you consistently respond with love in what you think, do and say, the two triangles will become one and you will experience peace and abundance in all areas of your life.

Keep this piece of paper with you at all times as

6   a reminder that you are love and also as a reminder
to extend that love to others.

Confucius wrote: "What the great man seeks is
in himself. What the small man seeks is in others."
So, look inside yourself and decide what you really
want from life. When you really become comfortable
with yourself, your material needs will all be met
and you can spread your inner peace to others, and
they, in turn, will spread theirs.

> It's never too late for you to re-examine your
> beliefs and values and make changes in your
> life—changes which allow love to flourish.

Unconditional Love

Here's an example of how powerful love can be.

My friend, Unity minister Eric Butterworth,
tells the story of a college professor whose sociology
class went into a slum area in Baltimore to get case
histories of 200 boys. The students were asked to
write an evaluation of each boy's future. In many
cases, the students wrote the boys didn't have a
chance because of their poverty.

Twenty-five years later, another professor came
across the study and decided to do a follow-up. To

his surprise, many of those boys had achieved more than ordinary success in law, medicine, business and so on. The professor questioned some of the men who still lived in the area about their success, and many of them attributed their achievements to their grade school teacher. Since the teacher was still alive, the professor got a chance to ask her about her secret. She told the professor, "It's really very simple, I loved those boys."

How wonderful that love found a way when there appeared to be none.

I once heard a woman recall a conversation with a person who was being very disrespectful. The woman decided to send mental love arrows straight at that individual. The more derogatory his remarks became, the more she kept visualizing and firing little love arrows at him. In just a short time the woman actually changed his attitude and their conversation was completely reversed into a pleasant exchange.

Again, love reversed a situation that many would have given up on.

It can.

It does.

It will.

That's the power of real love—it's *unconditional*. Most of the time when we love, we say, "I will love you if . . . It's love with strings attached. That's not love, that's bartering, exchanging one commodity for another. The type of love I'm talking about is a totally unconditional love: "I'll love you regardless of what you do." Unconditional love doesn't mean you allow a loved one to abuse you. You don't have to tolerate abuse from others, but you can still love and accept people for what they are. All you have to do is let go and stop trying to force others to behave the way you want. If you allow life to unfold, things will naturally fall into place.

I've had two powerful experiences in my life where I expressed unconditional love and witnessed its positive effects. The first was with my mother, Ruby. In her case, a long time passed before I really had an understanding of love. Growing up I regularly went to church where people talked about love. But I didn't come from an environment that demonstrated the type of caring we usually associate with love. My mother was a strict disciplinarian who whipped me unmercifully many times. With each stroke she would remark how whipping me hurt HER much more than it did ME. (I still have not figured that one out.) I didn't love my mother or her actions during those times.

As a result of my early childhood experiences,

my first two marriages failed because I didn't know how to give love. I was often cold to my wives because I didn't know how to be otherwise. With Ruby as my role model for love, I never learned how to be gentle.

Years later, I learned how to develop a mother-son relationship with Ruby when I stopped trying to change her. I learned that love doesn't mean changing someone. Love means accepting an individual exactly as he or she is.

My relationship with Ruby improved when I realized it was impossible for her to extend the type of love I looked for because she had not experienced it herself. My mother's life had been hard. She didn't grow up in a loving, nourishing environment. She never received much education and had to start work at a very early age. She worked as a domestic and she and my father fought much of the time. So, I forgave her for not loving me the way I thought she should, and started being more loving to her. I called her more often. In the past I would go for weeks without talking to her because she was always so negative. But I decided I could tune out the negative and lead the conversation into a more positive light. I started to be more positive and wouldn't give her the opportunity to be negative. I made a point of always telling her how much I loved her. I discovered firsthand, that love is nothing until you give it away—and then it's multiplied.

I made these adjustments not because I wanted Ruby to change, but because I realized that we are here to love one another. I simply loved my mother, and now she and I have a wonderful relationship. In many ways she's the same person, but it doesn't matter because I love her anyway.

Love changes your perception of another person; it changes your perception of life. Looking through the eyes of love, you'll find it impossible to pass judgments and see negatives about other people. Love is always giving and not expecting anything in return. That's when love is at its best. Teilhard de Chardin summed it up beautifully when he said: "Love alone is capable of uniting living beings in such a way as to complete and fulfill them, for it alone takes them and joins them by what is deepest in themselves."

My second experience with unconditional love happened with my youngest son, Shawn. By the time he reached the ninth grade his grades and behavior had sunk to a critical low. I thought it was time for Wally, the father, to step in and take charge. I had Shawn move from Los Angeles, where he was living with his mother, Shirlee, to Honolulu to live with me and my wife, Christine. I thought it was time for him to be under the influence of his father and by having him live with me I could have some control over his life. Boy was I wrong!

I was travelling a lot, so I still wasn't able to spend time with Shawn. Worse, I was trying to change him. I was attempting to persuade Shawn to be what I wanted him to be, rather than encouraging, supporting and letting him be himself. I became a father in the strictest sense—perhaps to the same degree that Ruby had been a mother to me. Shawn grew more distant, rather than closer to me.

Finally, he packed up and went back to live with his mother in Los Angeles. Over the next few months my son and I were at each other's throats. We would yell at each other over the telephone and he'd hang up on me. I felt totally frustrated. I saw myself as the martyred father trying to give my son everything I thought he needed and wanted. I saw myself as the victim. I turned to prayer and for the first time saw clearly that Shawn really was responsible for his life and that my responsibilities as his parent and guardian did not include molding him as I pleased.

Kahlil Gibran speaks eloquently of our children in his book, THE PROPHET: "And a woman who held a babe against her bosom said, 'Speak to us of

12   Children.' And he said: 'Your children are not your
     children.' They are the sons and daughters of Life's
     longing for itself.

     "They come through you but not from you, and
     though they are with you yet they belong not to
     you.

     "You may give them your love but not your
     thoughts, for they have their own thoughts.

     "You may house their bodies but not their souls,
     for their souls dwell in the house of tomorrow, which
     you cannot visit, not even in your dreams. You may
     strive to be like them, but seek not to make them
     like you."

     I saw Shawn reach the depths of despair and
     knew then that the best thing—really the only
     thing—I could do was to express the love I had for
     him. I let him know that I was there if he wanted to
     talk and that I would support and help him in
     positive ways any time and in any way I could.

     I learned that loving my son meant accepting
     his behavior and acknowledging his right to behave
     any way he wanted. I started loving Shawn no
     matter how he behaved. I began doing things to
     help him rather than saying, "You got yourself into
     this mess, now get yourself out." That's not love.
     Love is offering help and doing whatever is in your

power to assist family, friends or a lover in time of need and expecting nothing in return.

Once I let go of the desire to control Shawn and started loving him unconditionally, the pieces of the puzzle fell into place. Shawn began to make an incredible transformation—from shirking all responsibilities to becoming one hundred percent accountable for his actions. People began to come into his life to help him on his path and he began to respond to them.

After successfully completing his freshman year at Boston University, College of Communication, Shawn went on to become an active and enthusiastic film student at New York University Tish School of the Arts, which by the way was his first choice. I believe the outcome of my crisis with Shawn would have been drastically different if I hadn't shown him deep, unconditional love. For me, this was an unforgettable lesson in how absolutely overwhelming the power of love really is.

My friend Abdul Aziz Said introduced me to a writing by Ameen Rihani, a mentor of Kahlil Gibran, that speaks of unconditional love.

> My heart is the field I sow for you.
> For you to water and to reap
> My heart is the house I open for you.

14

For you to air and dust and sweep.
My heart is the rug I spread for you.
For you to dance or pray or sleep.
My heart is pearls I thread for you.
For you to wear, to break or to keep.

Love in Business

Are you one of those who believe that love can only be applied to personal situations and not to business? Well, I'm afraid I must disagree with you. My success in the cookie business is another great example of the power of love. Those little chocolate chip goodies are just the evolving vehicle on which I can spread my philosophies of peace and love. Let me go back for a moment and tell you about my first encounter with them.

When I was ten, my Aunt Della got me hooked on chocolate chip cookies while I was visiting her for the summer. I *loved* them. I'd sit around the house just waiting for them to come out of the oven. I was reunited with the delectable morsels when I moved into my aunt's small apartment in New York City several years later.

Years after that, besides my obsession with the marvelous taste and aroma, I found peace of mind whipping up batches of cookies that I baked and distributed everywhere I went. This worked wonders, especially in my career as a personal manager. The cookies' reputation began to grow as my contacts multiplied. People looked forward to those friendly, edible calling cards.

Can you see the love here? I *loved* the cookies my Aunt Della made for me. When she baked cookies and shared them, she was expressing her *love* for me and the rest of the family. When I began to bake them myself, it became my own creative project for the hour or so it took to mix the batter and pop 'em in the oven. At the time, my career wasn't going too well. I was an agent with the William Morris Agency and my clients were quitting the business or not paying me commissions. Once, a great prospect of mine literally broke his leg the first night of an out-of-town opening of a play we knew would be the springboard for his career. Baking cookies at home was my way of healing myself, *loving* myself and sharing my love with my friends.

When I finally entered the cookie business full time, I acknowledged to myself that I had taken a beating and that it was time for a change. If I could love myself once a week or so in my home kitchen, I thought, why couldn't I love myself full time, share that love with as many people as possible, and at the same time earn a living doing what I loved most, with a product I loved the best. "Famous Amos" became the vehicle to express my love in the outside world. The positive responses from the many people I've met through the years confirms that they felt my love. The reality is that I am in the people business, not the cookie business. And no matter what business *you're* in, you're in the people business, too. I deal in *love,* and so must you.

Since, for me, the bottom line in life and in business is people, it is important that they are nourished and feel loved. I often tell people that my cookies are made with love and since love is not fattening, Eat up! The people who make the cookies must feel loved also, so they can pass that love on while making the cookies. The customers must feel loved so they will become a friend of The Cookie and return for more. Never in my wildest dreams would I have thought I would gain so much insight into love through chocolate chip cookies, although now that I look back, it seems quite natural. For me, chocolate chip cookies have always been an expression of *love.*

Are you one of the many people with career complaints? Are you unhappy and thinking about starting a business or finding something more suitable? Would you like to improve your lifestyle, become rich and get off the treadmill?

> The key is not only LOVING what you do but
> BECOMING what you do.

I don't sell cookies, I *am* the cookie. My personality is part of that cookie; the cookie an extension of my personality. A good friend of mine, Lee Baby Simms, is a disc jockey, and when he's on the air he *is* the radio. Wayne Dyer, noted author and psychologist, says, "I am not a writer, I am writing. I *am* the words." You become what you do by loving what you do and it then becomes an extension of you.

If you find yourself involved in a job or in a work relationship that's uncomfortable, concentrate on the positive aspects of the situation. Stop dwelling on the negatives and find the positive elements. When you've identified what is positive and work on embellishing those areas, I'll bet all my cookies that you'll fall in *love* with them and the negatives will begin to dissolve. Keep in mind that whatever it is that you don't like was created by *you*. So you have the power to change it. It's as simple and as quick as *changing your mind*. Changing your mind is nothing more than making a decision or choosing to do something else. You do it all the time regarding minor issues. It could be as basic as deciding to wear

18 a different garment or changing one goal for another. Some decisions are more difficult and take longer than others, but all of life is just a series of decisions or choices. Why not apply that same concept to your work?

Perhaps the first step in beginning this process is to take a good look at why you feel you do not love some aspect of your job or someone you work with. Once you begin, you will see that the qualities you object to in others are really aspects of your own personality that you don't like. You'll see that you are lacking in love for yourself. How can you give someone or some task something you do not have? Life is a mirror; what you see lacking on the outside must first be lacking within. Changing jobs or co-workers will not always help, because everywhere you go you'll find *yourself*. Sooner or later you'll realize that the more positive energy, the more *love*, you give to your work and life in general, the more love and success you'll receive in return.

Learning to Love

Becoming a totally loving person is not easy. For me, it was a long process. I took no specific steps. Often I wasn't even conscious that I was changing. Many times I went kicking, screaming and resisting every step of the way. It doesn't have to take you as long as it took me. It can happen in a flash, the blink of an eye. But, because we're so resistant—our past experiences have been imprinted in our minds—it's difficult to change belief systems immediately. But just think, if you change now, you will have so much time to fully enjoy life. Don't be stubborn and fight it as I did. Accept love because sooner or later you'll realize that Emily Dickinson spoke the truth when she said: "All I know of love is that love is all there is."

By now you're probably wondering, "How can I become a more loving person?" Well, I don't have any quick solutions but I can share some of the things that worked for me in the hope that they will work for you.

One of the first things I did was become *more open-minded*. I quit thinking "I'm always right." I started to question some of my beliefs, some of my "truths." Where did these truths come from? Was that really how I felt? I began to see that some of the lessons I'd learned from childhood experiences were not valid. Some of my behavior was not in my best interest. I began to think there just might be another way of viewing the world. If you do nothing else, just think about that one possibility. Let the

20   possibility that there's another way of viewing the
world be a starting point for you.

Most importantly, open up to self-love. Develop love for yourself. Stop condemning yourself
and learn to love you as you are, even though you
might not like some of your physical features or
character traits. I acknowledge I can always improve,
but there is nothing *wrong* with me. If you're not
satisfied with certain of your attributes, develop a
program to change them. If you do something you
know isn't in your best interest or not at your highest
level of thinking, acknowledge that you have done
it, forgive yourself and move on.

> Love the inner you and keep moving ahead
> because you can't stand still and improve at the
> same time.

Don't be too hard on yourself. Know that you're
going to make mistakes, and realize that you'll grow
through them. If you didn't make mistakes you'd
stay at the same level of achievement and your life
would be very boring. Besides, there are really no
such things as mistakes—just learning experiences.

One of the major reasons my first two marriages
ended in divorce was because I had never really

experienced love. I never knew how to pass love on and share it with someone else. There were many times in my relationships with my first two wives when I just had to have my own way, even at the expense of hurting their feelings. Had I been at the level of understanding I am today, I would have been more loving and supportive, instead of greedy, deceitful and devious, faults that all come from fear and an absence of inner peace. At that time, I hadn't come to grips with knowing, loving and accepting myself. Therefore it was impossible for me to love anyone else.

So if you're wondering how you can be more loving, without a doubt the first step is to LOVE YOURSELF.

I'd like to share a little story with you called "IAM LOVE," a story of unconditional self-love.

IAM was a small, furry brown caterpillar sitting on a limb of a bush munching on a green leaf. He thought of himself as a very lowly, ugly creature and wondered why God had made him this way. He had all kinds of unloving thoughts about himself and others. Suddenly the thought came to him that perhaps he ought to try loving himself and others just to see what would happen. First, he washed himself in a little pool of water caught from a recent rain storm and brushed himself against the bark of a

22 tree. He looked bright and shiny and was surprised to find that other caterpillars came over to see him and tell him how nice he looked. Remembering that he had discovered a bush with an especially tasty leaf, he decided to make a special effort to find it again and even invited some of his friends to go along on the adventure. They sang and danced all along the way. They didn't find that particular bush but they did find other bushes with even tastier leaves.

Finally IAM grew very tired and he made himself a snug cocoon in which to take a long nap. When he woke up, he was very much surprised to find he had turned into a beautiful butterfly. He joined many other butterflies who were feeling a marvelous sense of peace, warmth and joy that they had never known existed. IAM had turned into perfect LOVE.

Next, you must share your perfect love with the rest of the world. How? First, *let go of judgment.* Judgment is like a screen or a wall between you and someone else.

It is impossible to love someone if you pass judgments on that individual.

You have already determined the type of person he or she is, but you don't really *know* the person. Preconceived judgments prevent you from ever seeing the real person. They stop you from getting to the soul of that individual, and then loving that soul. When you love a person, you separate the individual's actions from the individual. You do not have to love what a person does to love the person. We are more than our actions. Simply accept the actions and love the person.

I've mentioned fear as a factor that kept me from loving in my first two marriages. Love and fear cannot exist together. As Dr. Gerald Jampolsky says, "love is letting go of fear." Once you release your fears you're able to see clearly through the eyes of love. Fear immobilizes and prevents you from responding to life. Every time you feel fear creeping into your consciousness, let it dissolve. *Simply let fear go.*

A minister friend of mine, Phil Smedsted, once said: "Fear knocked at the door, faith opened the door and there was no one there." Faith is love at work in one's mind, so when you release all of your fearful thoughts of the future and replace them with loving thoughts of the present, you'll gradually see the whole pattern of your life change. Leo Tolstoy said: "Where there is faith, there is love; where

24   there is love, there is peace; where there is peace, there is God; where there is God, there is no need."

Another important step to take toward love is *to let go of expectations*. If you visualize what life should be and get bogged down with expectations it may be counterproductive. You set yourself up for a let down. You need flexibility. Visualizing your dreams and establishing goals for yourself produces results, but you must leave room for the unexpected. Let serendipitous experiences enter your life and you will profit from them. When you're a giving person and feel infinite love, it doesn't matter what the outcome of a situation is or what another person thinks or says, you're there to serve with no expectations, preconceptions or judgments.

Love in Relationships

What area of our life faces us with our greatest challenge? Our personal relationships. Love between two people. I can best illustrate that by talking about my relationship with my present wife, Christine. I've discovered that certain ingredients are required for building a sound and loving relationship. First, there has to be trust between two people. And there must be support. Give your loved one what that individual feels he or she needs, rather than what you *think* they need. Before I married Christine I reviewed my two previous marriages and realized I had always given what I had thought my wives needed, or what I wanted them to have, rather than what *they* wanted. You must give your mate a chance at self-expression. Don't write the script for your loved one's life. The other person is his or her own author. Besides, you are too busy writing the script for your own life. Together the two of you are co-authors of the script for your relationship. The relationship becomes the joint project in each of your lives in which you both contribute equally.

Christine and I work at our relationship as a constant, never-ending process of developing acceptance, unconditional love and self-love. A marriage, a relationship, does not stay fixed. As in everything else, there is change. The individuals involved must continually adapt to the most current needs of the relationship. Christine and I have grown together through our experiences with each other. Our love has developed out of a friendship that has deepened and deepened; and our friendship is stronger because of our love.

Another ingredient in creating a more loving relationship is desire.

> There must be a desire by each party to really make a relationship work. Without that desire, you'll unconsciously sabotage the relationship.

That's what happened with my first marriage. We were both going to counselling but I did not really have a desire to make the relationship work, so obviously it didn't.

Sometimes a fresh, outside opinion can straighten out or strengthen a relationship. Advice can come from a minister, psychologist, marriage expert or a good friend. Just about anyone you're comfortable with can help you to resolve your differences and initiate a healing process in the relationship.

Maturity has a lot to do with love and maintaining a loving relationship. Are you mature enough to put the needs of the relationship in front of your own personal needs? Or, are you being selfish in the relationship? For years, these were questions I refused to answer honestly. But over the years I've changed and that change has allowed me to be a loving person and undertake the responsibilities of a relationship.

Another personal experience that has helped me to understand unconditional love was the birth of Sarah, Christine's and my daughter. Sarah is definitely a product of the love in our relationship. The miracle of her birth affirmed my belief in myself, in God and love. Witnessing the birth of another human being is an awesome experience. You can't help feeling better about yourself.

Sarah weighed in as an 8 lbs., 8 oz. bundle of love. Now at 4½ years old, she is simply a bigger package of love. For as long as she lives, to me, she will never be less than love. As a child, she loves unconditionally, she does not hold grudges, she does not judge, she has no expectations on the world or her environment. She just loves. She has become my greatest teacher. In our hearts, we are all Sarahs. Though we've grown older, we are still love, but along the way we've added things that have confused us and covered up our core of love. We've added judgments, values and conditions on how we will give our love. All of these add-ons twist us around and prevent us from expressing what we truly are: packages of love.

There is a writing by Emmet Fox, a respected author and metaphysical minister, that sums up everything I've discussed in these many pages. It's called simply, "LOVE."

28

Love is by far the most important thing of all. It is the Golden Gate of Paradise. Pray for the understanding of love and meditate upon it daily. It casts out fear. It is the fulfilling of the Law. It covers a multitude of sins. Love is absolutely invincible.

There's no difficulty that enough love will not conquer; no disease that enough love will not cure; no door that enough love will not open; no gulf that enough love will not bridge; no wall that enough love will not throw down; no sin that enough love will not redeem.

It makes no difference how deeply seated may be the trouble, how hopeless the outlook, how muddled the tangle, how great the mistake; a sufficient realization of love will dissolve it all. If only you could love enough you would be the happiest and most powerful being in the world.

Many words have been written on love. However, no book has said it better than the Bible. From Corinthians, 13th chapter:

I may be able to speak the languages of men and even of angels, but if I have no love, my speech is no more than a noisy gong or a clanging bell. I may have the gift of inspired preachings: I may have all knowledge and understand all secrets; I may have all the faith needed to move mountains—but if I have no love, I am nothing. I may give away everything I have and even give up my body to be burned—but if I have no love this does me no good.

Love is patient and kind; it is not jealous or conceited or proud; love is not ill-mannered or irritable; love does not keep a record of wrongs; love is not happy with evil, but it's happy with the truth. Love never gives up and its faith, hope and patience never fail. Love is eternal.

The Bible says there are three attributes: faith, hope and love; and the greatest of these is love. So you see, God is love and you are created in his likeness and image: *you are love.*

2

THE
POWER
IN ATTITUDE

I am upset, not by events, but rather by the way I view them.

—Epictetus 1st Century A.D.

I suppose, in the early '60s I could have settled for becoming the first Black agent at a major theatrical agency and left my life's achievements at that. But considering what the opportunities had been prior to my breakthrough, the future didn't look that great for others to follow. That thought, along with the challenge of new ground yet to be conquered spurred me on to become the best agent I could. My attitude said, "Success does not come to you, you go to it."

Do you believe that the results in your life relate directly to your attitude? William James, the distinguished psychologist, said, "The greatest discovery of my generation is that human beings can alter their lives simply by altering their attitude." There truly is immense power in your attitude.

I was boarding a plane in Los Angeles, en route home to Honolulu, when I overheard a lady commenting on what a bad day she was having and how unlucky she was. I got into the conversation and suggested she stop confirming her bad luck. Her son, who was traveling with her, agreed, saying, "That's why she's so unlucky, she's always complaining about having bad luck." That woman clearly created her own bad luck with her negative attitude.

My experiences have taught me to shape my own life by changing my attitude about the world I live in.

> I've developed a positive mental attitude, which in turn has created a positive life.

For years I didn't know what I wanted to do with myself. I only knew what I did not want to do, how I did not want to do it, where I did not want to do it, and who I did not want to do it with. Living my life from such a negative perspective obviously produced negative results. I was not happy at home, when I was there, which wasn't often, and when away I constantly searched, and in all the wrong places, for my life's missing ingredients. I finally found what I had been looking for all those years. The answer lay inside me all along: a change of attitude. A positive attitude tells you that life is never really what it appears to be—it is always more. Let's examine attitude more closely and see how we actually do control our lives by controlling what we think and how we think about it.

The dictionary defines "attitude" as, a state of mind or feeling with regard to some matter; a second definition is, disposition. "Disposition" is defined as one's customary manner of emotional response, or temperament. "Temperament" is the manner of thinking, behaving or reacting characteristic of a specific individual. All of these definitions tell you that attitude is an inner experience. In that case, you and only you are responsible for your attitude. Your attitude is established by what you say and do. Your actions are determined by what you think. When you deny responsibility for your thoughts, you believe that the causes of events in your life are outside of you. When you live with that belief, that attitude, all you can do is react. You complain about

34   how "they treat me." You sit down and brood about
how "nothing good ever happens to poor me."

You can choose your feelings, your behavior,
your attitude. You can choose the results in your
life. You can begin to accept the responsibility of
your actions.

> Each of us has free will and we have chosen the
> results in our lives, either passively or actively.

That's an important aspect of our reality for us to
accept. It means that in every situation we encounter, we have a choice. I believe that the choice we
make is directly related to how responsible we are.
In fact, the word "responsible" means being able to
make moral or rational decisions on one's own and
therefore being accountable for one's own behavior.
Another definition is the ability to be trusted or
depended upon; to be reliable.

Can you begin to see the importance of a
positive mental attitude? How exactly do we go
about developing a positive mental attitude? If your
thoughts determine what you say and do, the first
action you need to take is to stop behaving like a
robot who can only do as others instruct. You must
begin to think for yourself.

> Thinking is the first act in creating your world
> as you want it to be.

You must monitor your thoughts. I actually started listening to my thoughts and questioning whether they were in my best interest or for my highest good. You must begin to question everything you come into contact with: that's how learning takes place. You must also monitor how you react to experiences and not get into the habit of automatically rejecting something just because it is different or unfamiliar. Once you have opened yourself to new and different experiences, good begins to come into your life in new shapes; shapes that a limited, negative attitude would have rejected before realizing any of the rewards involved. This really is the process I used to improve the quality of my life. The change means dismantling the wall that an old attitude has placed in front of your objective mind. When we make a commitment to change our attitudes, we begin in a very real sense a process of unlearning all the stuff we thought was best for us. As you strip away layers and layers of negative attitudes and replace them with positive attitudes, your horizon broadens and

36   your capabilities increase. You go to success, success does not come to you.

Attitude Precedes Circumstance

Are you one of the many who believes you must first receive the desired results in your life before establishing a positive attitude to go along with your new status? That's putting the plow before the horse. Attitudes are never a result of circumstances. Circumstances are the result of attitudes. I agree wholeheartedly with George Bernard Shaw who said, "I don't believe in circumstances. The people who get on in the world are those who get up and look for the circumstances they want."

> Success is the result of an attitude that can find the positive, worthwhile aspects of everything it comes into contact with and denies anything that may be negative or hindering.

If I did not first have a positive attitude and believe I could open a store selling chocolate chip cookies, there is absolutely no way I could have opened my first store. When I reflect on my achievements, I recognize that they all result from maintaining a positive mental attitude.

For example, I started my adult working life as a part-time stock clerk in the supply department of Saks Fifth Avenue in New York City and advanced to manager in two short years. That happened only because I gave more than I was asked or expected to give, and I gave it in a cheerful manner. Then in 1961, feeling there was more to life than the supply department of Saks, I resigned without having another job, even though my wife was pregnant with our second child. I later joined the William Morris Theatrical Agency as a messenger in the mail room and in less than one year became an agent. All this happened because I had a positive, friendly, cheerful attitude about the work I did and always showed a willingness to learn more and accomplish more. Positive work ethics show people that you do not fear work and that you can handle the responsibilities that go along with the work. (There's that word again: responsibility.) In the job market that means advancement and increases in salary. In life in general it means achievement and success. Where would I be today if, as a stock clerk, I did my job grudgingly, with the attitude that said I was only going to do enough to get by and nothing more? You

38   can be sure I would *not* be enjoying the success I
enjoy today as Famous Amos.

> Create the circumstances you want in your life
> right now by developing a positive mental atti-
> tude.

A positive attitude says success is a journey, not
a destination. With a positive attitude you know
that throughout each day you experience success.
During the early years of the cookie business, people
often asked me how it felt to finally be a success.
They unconsciously implied that, for thirty-nine
years, prior to my selling cookies I had been a
failure. Perhaps they too were not feeling successful
and wanted to know how it felt. My response was
always a positive, "I've never been a failure. With
each attempt I learned something new that moved
me just a little closer to my goal." Dr. George
Sheehan said, "Success rests with having the courage
and endurance and, above all, the will to become
the person you are, however peculiar that may be.
Then you will be able to say, I have found my *hero*
and he is me." Life never fails and it never goes
backwards. A positive attitude helps you to see that

more clearly. A positive attitude also lets you see that you are the star and the real *hero* of your life.

A positive mental attitude will lead you to strong self-esteem, pride in yourself, and you will constantly project love, understanding, patience, confidence and all the wonderful characteristics we all inherently possess.

Your positive attitude alone will create that type of environment around you; attitude creates your reality.

In this respect attitude could very well be the most important aspect of our lives.

A friend of mine, Steve Crothers, calls attitude the "Magic Word." It's important to realize, though, that *you* create the magic that makes your attitude work. That's what it's all about. When you start thinking in a positive manner, you will realize that the actions, feelings and moods you project bring out the reactions, moods and feelings of the people you come into contact with. And of course, that works both ways. How often are you rude to a person because they were rude to you? A person with a positive attitude must challenge him or herself to stay positive all the time. Practice returning that coarse "Watch it buddy or you'll get yours," with, "Please excuse me and have a nice day." A positive attitude can change the negative around it into positive also. Our actions, feelings and moods definitely create the texture of our immediate environment.

If you think you're out there all alone, maintaining a positive attitude about life can be a lost battle. Acknowledging that a higher power exists for you to work with can remove the fear. Personally, I know now that my life constantly flows and is shaped in positive ways through the guidance of that higher power. Whether you call it God, Allah, Buddha or "Larry" does not matter. The importance lies in the faith and acceptance placed in that force. Armed with that kind of faith, you will find it impossible *not* to keep a positive attitude about all of life's adventures.

One of the first areas I applied my new-found understanding of life was to my relationship with my wife, Christine. Instead of focusing on things I didn't like in our relationship, I began to pay attention to those things I liked and worked on changing my attitude about those I didn't. As I discussed in the chapter on love, I developed the attitude that I should be giving Christine what she wanted, not what I wanted her to have. Neither of us is an expert, and we are practicing daily. Yet, because of our positive attitude, our relationship continues to improve.

One realization I've gained from having a positive attitude is that I am perfect just *as* I am, right *where* I am. Accepting myself right now, as I am, enables me to assess every aspect of me and make changes in those areas that are less than I desire. As I mentioned earlier, life is never really what it seems, it is always more. Therefore, you are never really what you seem, you are always more.

> A positive mental attitude not only helps you to visualize what you want to be, it helps you become it.

The First-Rate Attitude

How can you be first-rate? You can't if you use second-rate ingredients in your life. A positive attitude helps you constantly attract the very best of everything into your life.

42   When I decided to open a store selling only chocolate chip cookies, I also decided to sell the best tasting, highest quality, cutest, most adorable, chocolate chip cookies that I possibly could. I made a conscious commitment to excellence and quality. I refused to use second-rate chocolate simply because everybody else did. The fact that in my opinion everybody else used second-rate ingredients was the reason no other chocolate chip cookie satisfied me. My goal was to make a homemade-tasting cookie, which would be different from anything that was currently being sold. I knew I could not do that by using the same ingredients everyone else used. My positive attitude acted as a watchdog that permitted nothing but the best in my cookies.

History has shown that people are capable of producing results far and above the norm. You must commit to what at first may seem impossible and be willing to "go for it" totally, no matter how long it may take. An affirmation my friend Ken Malach shared with me will help keep your eye on the goal. "I believe that if I give my best, and we do our best, we shall be the best." That thought acknowledges that everything starts with *self*, then spreads to the whole. And I am reminded of a thought another friend Rozzell Sykes shared with me: "While everyone else is doing their worst, I will continue to do my best." So in everything you do, be the best. Develop a consciousness of "I can" and "I will." Think about your chosen task in those terms instead of automatically saying: "This is going to be difficult," or "I don't know if I can do that." Let your positive attitude help you achieve the perfection that is your birthright.

> Believe that you can and you take the first step toward completing any task.

The same holds true if what you want is a positive attitude. There are several ways I've developed a positive attitude in my life. Practice applying these concepts to your own situations. Again, if they work for me, they will also work for you.

How to Adopt a New Attitude

Accept the present and let go of the past. Many times we deny reality or attempt to hold on to past realities. How can change possibly take place when we hold on to past images, pretending the present ones do not exist. An attitude of acceptance and letting go helps us find the positive aspects of the reality we cannot change, embellishes them, then transforms what's left. A person with an accepting attitude does not get depressed because of a rainy day, but rather acknowledges rain as a necessary element of life. An accepting attitude says that, "When life gives you lemons, make lemonade!" Make the most of what you've got. You will not be able to appreciate more in your life until you learn to appreciate what you currently have. Do and give your best now.

We've all heard the proverbial quote, "Is the glass half-full or half-empty?" This illustrates better than anything I've seen that attitude is a matter of perspective. A positive attitude emphasizes perseverance over a challenge that may seem insurmountable. A positive attitude places more importance on the means than on the end. A positive attitude also focuses on the solution and not on the problem. If you go through the day doing your best possible, at the day's end you will look back and marvel at all you've accomplished.

You might as well live in the present because the past is gone and the future is not ready to be acted upon. Nine-tenths of the worries in an average life concern the future. The remaining one-tenth is probably about the past.

> When we live in the present, we live a longer, happier and more useful life. Be your best *today*. He who gives his best today will be even better tomorrow.

People constantly ask me what my secret is. If I had any secrets, one of them surely would be living in the present. That's how I live my life. Through experience, I've learned that a positive today is the closest think you can get to a secure tomorrow. Giving your best today does not necessarily guarantee you there will be a tomorrow. But if tomorrow *does* come you will be much better prepared to deal with it having lived a positive today. Let me pass on to you a piece I discovered in a Unity publication: It speaks squarely to the issue of living in the present.

"Today Is Yours"
by Coletta Davidson

"Today is the full bloom of life: The petals of yesterday have shriveled in the past; tomorrow is an unopened bud that may be blackened by the frost or beautified by the sun of life.

46

"The future is but a seed, not yet planted, of unknown quality; but today—today is a gorgeous blossom of beauty and fragrance.

"Today is a new page in the book of life. Upon it and upon it alone, you can write a record of your accomplishments; but once turned, it is gone forever.

"Yesterday is a page turned; you cannot add one line to it or erase one word from it. It is closed forever and can affect the new page only insofar as it has affected your heart and courage.

"Your mistakes and fears of yesterday need not be carried forward in the ledger of life. The past holds no mortgage on tomorrow.

"Today is yours, an immeasurable treasure, a house of golden opportunities, a sea of unfathomed possibilities, a forest of building prospects. Today is the clear note and the beautiful blossom in your song of time.

"There are hours in each day for work, for play, for meditation, for friends, loved ones, and rest. No one knows the limits of accomplishments.

"Today is yours. Use it for the full bloom of life."

Entwined with acceptance and life in the now is *forgiveness*. If an event has already happened, you can do nothing about it. Acceptance becomes the best response. If someone did something to you or you did it to yourself, forgiveness is the best response. Holding a grudge against that person or against yourself will keep you from surmounting that challenge. When you let go and forgive you can grow from the experience: you become understanding of the other side and can learn from that perspective.

The healing of my relationships with my mother and my youngest son, Shawn, had a lot to do with attitude and forgiveness. For a long time, I had an attitude of contempt for my mother because she did not treat me and love me the way I thought she should. I allowed that unforgiving attitude to interfere with the love I had for her. By changing my attitude from one of negative contempt to that of positive, unconditional love, I finally learned to accept her the way she is and just love her anyway.

When I made my son Shawn move to Hawaii, I had the attitude of a disciplinarian who sought domination over his life. That attitude prevented the development of a harmonious father-son relationship. I had created a relationship based on control instead of love. In response, Shawn developed an attitude of resentment and rebellion. Our attitudes became walls through which neither of us could see what the other truly wanted and needed.

48   Shawn needed love and support from me. When I let go of my attitude of authority I could see his needs, to which I began to respond. When he saw that I wanted to help and had stopped seeking to control, his resentment dissolved. He began to return my love and support with love and respect, which had been what I tried to force from him. This happened because of forgiveness. Had Shawn not been able to forgive me, he would have continued to rebel against my actions. If I had not forgiven him, I would never have allowed him to help himself. We both would still be entwined in a blind circle of reactions to negative attitudes. Let go of your negative attitudes, develop a positive attitude and you develop a clear perception of your position in your world.

What has worked exceptionally well for me is this: create a cheerful world for yourself; *be happy and have fun.*

We have already established that in life we all have a choice. Why not choose to be happy, regardless of what comes? It is really the only choice to make. Think of everything as joy, knowing that like attracts like. The depressed mind is always dull and never sees anything clearly. The cheerful or happy mind learns more rapidly, remembers more easily, understands more perfectly. Why not choose to be happy? I'll tell you a real secret. *It's okay to have fun.* During a promotion in a department store I went running through the store yelling: "It's okay to have fun, it's okay to have fun!!" People looked at me like I was crazy. I didn't let that stop me. I went right on having fun. Do you secretly believe that life is not fun? How many times a day do you stop yourself from doing something that you think would really be fun to do? Too many people wrap themselves up in seriousness. My motto is, *I'm not serious, but I am responsible.* You can be responsible and still have fun. The serious people judge the world as wrong and then try to fix it. People with a happy, positive attitude accept the world as it is and say, "How can I make this better." When all is said and done, life becomes the attitude with which you live it. You and *only you* create the pictures that become your world.

Here's one last analogy of how attitude works: If you were in a theater watching a movie, and about a quarter of the way through you decided it wasn't a movie you liked or wanted to see, what would you do? Throw tomatoes at the movie screen and yell obscenities, or leave the theater and go to see another movie? Even though the latter would be better than throwing tomatoes at the screen, it would not change the image. Or would you go to the projection room and give the projectionist a different reel of film to show? The point is, you can't change the image shown on the screen by tearing down the screen. In order to change the image, you must change the film in the projector. Life works the same way and you are the projector.

> Whatever you see on the screen of life was first seen in your mind. If you don't like what you see, change the reel of film, change your attitude, change your thoughts. Change your thoughts and you change your world. You are the power.

My experiences have shown me that a positive mental attitude says, My goal is not to *set* things right, but to *see* them rightly. That's what I did with Ruby and Shawn. I began to look at them as they were, not as I wanted them to be. I love my friend Jerry Jampolsky's quote, "Do I want to be right, or do I want to be happy?" What do *you* want to be?

Take it from a guy who's tried to do both and discovered peace of mind in finally being happy. Choose happy and quit trying to be right. Our attitude is the by-product of our thoughts. It is in our attitude that we discover strength or weakness, hope or anxiety, determination or frustration.

Give your life a boost today.

Develop a positive mental attitude.

3

THE
POWER
IN SELF-ESTEEM

You are an Individual Expression of God

How high is your self-esteem? How many times a day do you even give self-esteem any thought? If your answers are on the negative side, I want to help you make them more positive. In this chapter, I want to help you raise your level of self-esteem by exploring with you the power in a strong self-image based on self-esteem.

First off, let's dissect it. "Self-esteem": esteem of self; holding your self in high regard. "Esteem"

54   means to think favorably of; to consider valuable. So, self-esteem is thinking of yourself as a valuable entity.

When did you first hear the words self-esteem or the term self-image? I must have been in my late forties when I started hearing conversations focusing on such words. I had just begun attending a Unity Church in Hawaii where the minister dealt with teaching people how fantastic they really are.

When I was growing up, everybody talked about the exact opposite. Whenever I expressed positive thoughts as a child, I heard the "who-do-you-think-you-are-and-what-makes-you-so-high-and-mighty" lecture. After years of being told how selfish and egotistical I acted I developed an inferiority complex and low self-esteem. Many people who have a poor self-image blame childhood experiences and claim that their low self-esteem was reinforced by environment, family or acquaintances. While there is some degree of truth in that, I believe it is always done with the permission of the individual. Free will and free choice make us one hundred percent responsible for our self-image. Through the years I have been able to build my self-esteem by self-examination and a strong desire to take responsibility for my life.

Sometimes we don't exercise those options.

When we allow ourselves to be dominated by the decisions of others, we feel better believing that no choice existed. We live much of our lives based on the opinions of others.

> When we refuse to think, we allow others to create our own opinions of ourselves.

We permit others to build or destroy our self-images. These negative opinions become anchors that weigh us down and prevent us from soaring as God meant us to. The anchors are "I can't," "I wish," and "I would, but . . ."

An example: For forty-some years I never learned how to swim. Every time I was confronted with the opportunity to swim, I would respond, "I can't swim." The true response should have been, "I've never learned how to swim."

Every time I said "I can't," it made me feel insufficient. I compared myself to others who could swim and judged them as superior to myself because they had a skill I had never taken the time to learn. Saying "I can't" induces a sense of ineptness. The "I can't" in one area even triggers "I can't" in other areas of your life. I can't get a job, I can't get a girlfriend or boyfriend. All of these "can'ts" add up and become, "I can't do anything," followed by deep depression and further damage to your self-image and self-esteem. Instead of saying "I can't," say, "I've never learned how."

One day I said, "I've never learned how to swim." And you know what? I learned. Then I discovered that by practicing, my swimming can improve. Needless to say, my self-image and self-esteem improved also. I learned a very important lesson by learning to swim: I can do anything I set my mind to. I need only make the effort and trust the creative force or spirit within me. The important thing is to work constantly on motivating yourself to do things you once thought you couldn't do. Watch your self-esteem soar. Remember, your self-image and self-esteem are created by your belief system, which can be falsely shaped by yourself and other people. When we permit others to create our self-images, we discount our ability to learn. So your goal is to build a positive belief system.

You're a Piece of Work

People spend millions of dollars for great masterpieces and one-of-a-kind collector's items, but how often do we see ourselves as masterpieces or one-of-a-kind collector's items? Thinking of yourself as a masterpiece or a collector's item can be the starting point of building your self-esteem. Let's examine a few of the marvelous components that make you a very unique human being. Consider your eyes. The millions of receptors in your eyes enable you to see all of the wonders God has created: sunrises (as I write, I am experiencing the most incredible sunrise), sunsets, seasonal changes from the mist on a crisp winter day to flower buds breaking through the soil in spring, rising heat on those dog days of summer, the bursts of brilliant color changes in the fall, and the smile of a friendly face. Your eyes are also fountains pouring outward. They allow you to superimpose the attitudes you create in your mind onto the world outside. So much that you see out there is attitude; the world becomes what you want to see.

Another organ many people take for granted is the heart. The "star of the show." Your heart pulsates thirty-six million beats a year—year after year, night and day. That muscle pumps your blood through more than sixty thousand miles of veins, arteries and capillaries. Your heart pumps more than six hundred thousand gallons of blood through those vessels each year. It even combats stress unless con-

58 tinuously overtaxed. No one has been able to create a machine to equal the human heart and I venture to say no one ever will.

Sitting on top of your shoulders, directing and controlling the entire show, is the most complex of computers—your brain. It weighs only three pounds, yet it contains thirteen billion nerve cells—the most complex filing system known to man. Implanted within your brain cells are billions upon billions of protein molecules recording your every perception of sound, taste, smell, your every action and experience since your day of birth. Your every experience, even going back *before* birth, stays with you, registered in your brain, awaiting instant recall.

Connected from your brain throughout your body are four million pain-sensitive structures, five hundred thousand touch detectors and more than two hundred thousand temperature detectors. Your brain dispenses medication far more powerful than any doctor could ever prescribe. All positive and negative thoughts that control your outlook on life originate in your brain.

Tally all this up, add an entire reproductive system that can produce a human being, add a personality, emotions, fingers that can touch an apple, a tongue that can taste it, and what you get equals all of you. Each of us is made up of the same stuff, yet each of us is unique. We have so much to be proud of; our self-esteem should be sky-high.

Have you ever noticed how people pull each other down? We shouldn't. We are all valuable because we are all created with the element of greatness. Discard the "small self" so often seen and get in touch with the "magnificent self" that was meant to excel; that magnificent self created to invent airplanes, build cities, harness lightning, cure the sick; the same magnificent self that has written great music, plays, books and movies. Realize that all great scientists, inventors, playwrights, sports figures, business tycoons, political leaders and all others viewed as special are no more special than you and me. They were born with the same equipment—lungs, heart, eyes, ears, brains—that you and I have.

From this second on, know that you too are special and capable of achieving great things. To prove it to yourself start listing your assets—the ones God gave you, not the ones you can buy with money. You have enough assets to create anything in your world you desire with a lot left over to share. You can begin the list with the parts of your body, but it goes far beyond that.

60   Think of self-esteem in terms of love. Love yourself!!

> Treat yourself with love as an individual expression of God, as a priceless work of art.

Love is important to self-esteem. You've got to be able to love yourself before you can love anything or anyone else. To love yourself you must think of you as an object worthy of your own love. Love and self-esteem are principles intertwined.

> Start identifying your own unique characteristics. Each day work on finding new ones. Write them down and continue to reaffirm them.

"I am a kind person." "I serve the community by volunteering three hours a week," and so on. Whatever it is you have and do, remains individual to you. Claiming it will definitely improve your self-esteem, and you will begin to recognize that you are worthy of your own love.

Through Literacy Volunteers of America I've

met many adults who thought they couldn't read because they had teachers and parents who weren't supportive and who called them stupid or told them they couldn't learn. These false beliefs intensified over the years and prevented these adults from ever learning to read and also created learning disabilities in other areas of their lives. But through Literacy Volunteers of America and other groups that are working to wipe out illiteracy, people are proving they can learn to read and achieve success at other things as well. I've had tutors tell me that teaching someone to read is like watching flowers bloom right before their very eyes. Once these adults learn to read, other *"I can'ts"* in their lives disappear. They begin to develop a better self-image. And it doesn't matter how old you are. I met Sallie Williams in a reading program in Council Bluffs, Iowa; she was 100 years old and just learning how to read.

Everything begins with self-esteem, everything—a fantastic job, excellent health, a great marriage and family life. If you think nothing of yourself you will never aspire to obtain anything of worth for yourself. Many people have more respect for Rembrandts and Picassos than for themselves. But we human beings are the real masterpieces. Any one of us is infinitely more important than a mere

62 painting on a piece of canvas. Pope John Paul II once said, "The value of a man isn't measured by what he has, but by what he is." When a person has self-esteem, he or she can build outward into the world and create works of art, just as Rembrandt and Picasso did. You're Worth It

Most of us hold within us the unspoken and perhaps even unacknowledged notion that we do not deserve all the things we want. How absurd! Of course we're worthy; actually, we are meant to have everything our hearts desire. Why should we be able to dream of something if we are not worthy of having it. If we can't have or do what we think, we never would have thought of it. Believe me, we *all* are worthy.

In addition to sparking us on to achieve for ourselves, our self-image can be a starting point toward resolving the world's difficulties. Think big! It can happen. To bring about world peace, think of yourself as an individual worthy of living in a peaceful world.

Your attitude toward your world hinges on how you look at yourself. The world outside becomes a reflection of what you are within.

I've read studies which show the development of self-esteem reduces drug abuse and teen pregnancy while increasing academic achievement and social responsibility. Can you see how self-esteem, or the lack of it, can influence those four areas of indulgence? When people have little or no self-esteem and don't see themselves as being worth the investment of energy and time, they do things that remove themselves from the realm of positive social activity. They drink or take drugs in an attempt to block out the outside world, which they see as a dangerous and harmful place. They forget who they are because they don't think of themselves as a person who deserves much consideration. With a negative self-image, you treat yourself harmfully and allow negative things to happen to you. Those negative feelings radiate outward in the shape of harmful actions against the closest object, usually a loved one.

The result of high levels of self-esteem is an increased investment in self because you finally firmly believe you're worth it. The power of self-esteem is the power to grow, exist and serve positively.

Remember, you choose how you see yourself. When you decide to accept the truth of your being— that you were conceived in greatness—those anchors of "I can't" and other negative thoughts are removed

64 and you begin a life of peace accompanied by fulfillment and achievement.

How many people in your life can help you improve your self-esteem? Only you. An affirmation that might help realize this is, "If it is to be, it is up to me." Those ten two-letter words contain a large degree of truth. Take charge of your life and replace your negative habits with positive ones. Stop being a victim who blames others or the past for your dissatisfaction. Take responsibility for your world.

What kinds of results are you getting now? Are you happy? Are your relationships working? Do you have enough money? Are you living the life you *really* want to live? If not, something's wrong with your thought process because *you* create the world you live in.

Physical appearances, or what we *perceive* our physical appearances to be, have a direct effect on our self-image and self-esteem. There was a time when I did not like my physical appearance. I wanted to look like the TV and movie star images that Hollywood and advertisers had created, even though they were all white and there was no way I could change the color of my skin. I could, however, change the way I felt. I began to do that by standing in front of the mirror and concentrating on how I looked physically. I decided what I considered attractive about myself. I kept reminding myself that this was all I had to work with, so I'd better learn to like it.

I noticed my eyes were friendly and that I had a great smile. The more I learned to admire my features, the more my self-esteem rose. Use this system for *your* self-improvement. It works. All you're doing is concentrating on the positive.

As a boy growing up in Tallahassee, Florida, I was not encouraged in this type of thinking. Nobody ever told me of my inherent greatness, and how much potential I had. When I moved to New York City as a teenager, I felt like a country boy moving to the big city. I *was* a country boy moving to the big city. I felt I couldn't compare with all of the big, streetwise guys. I belittled myself because I was skinny. How skinny? Well, if I turned sideways and stuck out my tongue I'd look like a zipper. I remember as youngsters, my best friend, Walter Carter, and I lifted weights in the hope of getting muscles like Charles Atlas, the macho hero-figure of the day. We thought of ourselves as the skinny guys, portrayed in the Charles Atlas body-building ads, who always got sand kicked in their faces.

My transformation started after I got out of the

Air Force. In my twenties, I began to accept my body and the fact that it was okay to be skinny. As a matter of fact, I discovered it was actually healthier. I didn't physically change but instead, and more importantly, I changed my attitude. By accepting my body, I reinforced my self-worth, and stopped my self-hate and self-condemnation. You can't accept and hate or condemn at the same time.

Acceptance is a powerful tool in overcoming a low self-image.

Once you have learned acceptance, you can gently change any part of yourself without put-down, and further strengthen your self-esteem.

Until I began this process I was a shy, introverted guy. I feared asking a girl out for a date. I never learned how to dance, and rather than learn how to dance, I saw it as a big disadvantage. When I started dating my first wife, I felt perhaps I wasn't as outclassed by those other guys as I had once thought.

My self-image picked up even more after I got a job at the William Morris Agency, the largest theatrical agency in the world. After my initial training period, I got my business cards and discovered I could even impress people. But deep inside I still had a lot of second thoughts. The problem was that I impressed people with what was on the surface: my new show business career. I still didn't have the self-esteem to back up the business cards. In two marriages and numerous relationships I felt I could attract the ladies because of my career at William Morris, not because of Wally Amos. It takes some of us a long time to discover we are more than our title or our career.

In 1978, I began to get in touch with my inner self and view life from a spiritual perspective through the teachings of a Unity Church in Hawaii. This was the turning point. I started reading inspirational and motivational books that made me realize I had not been thinking. I was just *going* through life, instead of *growing* through life. I was replaying those past teachings of inferiority. When I began to let go of negative attitudes and old belief systems and analyze my actions and thoughts, I discovered how detrimental the past can really be. So, I started to let go and began exploring my possibilities.

Laugh Your Way to Greatness

Humor has played a vital role in helping me build my self-esteem. I'm able to laugh at myself during both the good and bad times. There were bad times like the period in my life when I wore only wash and wear clothes because I couldn't afford dry cleaning. I never wore socks because that was one area where I could cut back and save. I remember once being with a client, Franklyn Ajaye, who also did not wear socks, when Richard Pryor commented, "I see your socks match your gloves." I laughed as much as everyone else. I've discovered that if I make fun of me first, it reduces the importance of the moment.

Being able to laugh at myself also helps me be more compassionate.

> Self-esteem is based on self-compassion. If you can see the humor in something you've done, you can forgive yourself and move on.

When I started in the cookie business the emphasis was on comedy. I intended to make people laugh. To make myself laugh. In order to do that I often acted silly. Sometimes I'd wear silly caps, fluorescent socks or whatever made me feel good. I started playing the kazoo because it's humorous and fun. (I proclaimed the kazoo as the official instrument of The Cookie. No other cookie company has an official instrument.) I don't care if people think I'm stupid or silly, because I think well of myself. I have a positive self-image. I know I'm not stupid and it's okay to be silly. I am often reminded of Terry Cole Whitaker's book, *What You Think Of Me Is None Of My Business*. It's a great title and a very valuable book with a worthwhile message.

Humor disarms a person. It's impossible for someone to be angry with you if you create a humorous situation. There's no defense for it. As Famous Amos I've been able to inspire and motivate people while laughing and having a good time.

Take inventory of the things you do well and praise yourself for those achievements and you build self-esteem. The self-commendations can relate to your job. Congratulate yourself because you get in on time, or because you work well with your fellow employees. Mothers and housewives, or househusbands, your self-worth should be sky high because running a household and raising children are truly noteworthy achievements. Remember, it's important

70   *not* to compare yourself with others. You are a unique human being and your accomplishments are personal and uniquely yours. By taking a look at your accomplishments and the things you do well, you might find something that you can turn into a business as I did with chocolate chip cookies.

Every time you endorse your achievements, you build self-confidence.

We all want to be perfect. We are so quick to condemn ourselves for having faults. Faults are something that every human being has. They are a means for us to improve ourselves. In that respect, we are perfect because we have the means to improve. Just as you learn to accept your physical features and your body, you must also learn to accept your faults. Realize that you have the power to change them, but not until you accept their existence can you effect that positive change. Don't forget, as a child of God you have tremendous potential to change. Humor can help you accept a fault while you work on changing it.

It's also important to let go of guilt if you want to improve your self-esteem and self-image. It's time to wipe the slate clean. Whatever you've done in the past is over. Humor can help here, too. Smile about the past; no matter how bad it was, it's over now, and that's something to laugh about! Start living your life fresh from this moment on. Remember the saying, "Today is the first day of the rest of your life." It's necessary to do that in order to enhance your self-image. Don't wait for someone else to forgive you. At every stage of your life you were doing the best you could at the time.

So, forgive yourself.

Self-Esteem, In Short

Here are some things to keep in mind that will boost your self-image. Be good to yourself. Treat yourself generously. Sometimes we treat others better than we treat ourselves. Start treating yourself the way you want others to treat you. Visualize what you want from life and don't deny yourself that goodness. Every now and then, go out and buy yourself a present. Do something nice for yourself like taking a nice bubble bath rather than a quick shower. Allow some private time for yourself, regardless of your hectic schedule. You're the greatest person in your life, so take the time to appreciate you. When you start appreciating yourself like the special person you are, you'll feel better about yourself. And that's where self-esteem begins.

> Stop being your enemy and start being your friend. Don't pull yourself down, build yourself up. Begin to be truthful to yourself. Respect yourself, and hold the person you are in high value.

Empower yourself through prayer. Prayer gives you direct access to those infinite forces that created you. Tap into that power and you can't help but grow and feel proud of that growth.

Give to yourself enthusiastically. Treat yourself with generosity. Forgive yourself completely. Balance yourself harmoniously. Trust yourself confidently and completely. You know what's right and best for you. Listen to your small inner voice, don't ignore its urgings.

Above all, love yourself wholeheartedly and express that love in radiance. When you are able to get in touch with these feelings every day without effort, you will have attained a high level of self-esteem and you will have developed a positive self-image. Just remember, you're working to improve you. And what person in your life is worth working on more? What better gift to give yourself than a positive self-image and high self-esteem? Take good care of yourself. You're important to the entire world, but more importantly you are important to YOU.

4

THE
POWER
IN COMMITMENT

Today is worth two tomorrows

To commit or to proscrastinate? That is the question. Whether to make a decision to create a rich abundant life filled with the desires of your heart or to live a life of defeat and lack? Why is it that some people are successful and others never attain their goals? What do you suppose is the secret ingredient that pushes some over the top while others never even begin the climb? The largest obstacle between you and your goal is a lack of *total commitment*. Often we use phrases like, "I'll try," "I guess I can," "I hope I can." But commitment is expressed in two words: I WILL.

My personal struggles and experiences over the years have proven without a doubt that commitment gets the job done. Commitment is what separates the achievers from the sustainers. It was my unwavering commitment to open a store selling chocolate chip cookies that enabled me to give birth to the Famous Amos family of cookies.

Before going any further let me share with you a writing by the great German writer, Goethe. It is titled "The Power of Commitment."

Until one is committed, there is hesitancy, the chance to draw back, always ineffectiveness. Concerning all acts of initiative (and creation), there is one elementary truth the ignorance of which kills countless ideas and splendid plans: that the moment one definitely commits oneself, then providence moves too.

All sorts of things occur to help one that would never otherwise have occurred. A whole stream of events issues from the decision, raising in one's favor all manner of unforseen incidents and meetings and materials assistance, which no man could have dreamed would have come his way.

Are you in earnest? Seek this very minute, whatever

you can do, or dream you can, begin it. Boldness has genius, power and magic in it. Only engage and the mind grows heated, begin and then the task will be completed.

If you have never taken inventory of your life, now might be a good time to do so. How many times have you tried something without successfully completing it? What was your attitude at the time? Did you doubt your ability to perform? Did you doubt the credibility of your idea? Did you check with friends and relatives for their approval? What was your level of commitment? These are all symptoms of a person who has not made a total commitment to a goal. Perhaps you even said "yes" and then later decided it was a foolish idea or too risky. The point is, you never gave birth to your idea, and I'll bet you dollars to cookies a lack of total commitment played a big part in causing you to fall short of your goal.

I saw a series of illustrations entitled: "It Was Just an Idea," which further illustrate how crippling procrastination or lack of commitment can be. Immediately below the title were nine squares, each with a picture of a light bulb and a quote above each bulb.

1. The first square contains a brightly glowing bulb with the quote "I have an idea."

2. The bulb in square two has lost some of its glow and says, "A word of caution."

3. Square three has a dimmer bulb with the words, "A little too radical." Can someone really determine if something is too radical for you? Isn't that a decision only you can make?

4. In the fourth square the bulb continues to fade with the quote, "I like it myself but." "But" is one of the smallest words in the English language, yet it has become the biggest obstacle for so many people. "But" has probably killed more great ideas than any other word in the English language. Do yourself a favor, eliminate "but" from your vocabulary. You will achieve a lot more.

5. The fifth square shows the bulb darker yet and reads, "We tried something just like that once." They tried something just like that *once*. When you are committed, you make the effort over and over again. Commitment is the foundation on which determination and perseverance are laid. It's also important to realize that you have a different energy, spirit and creativity than anyone else. Even though many may have attempted and failed at an idea, *you* might succeed because the idea was just waiting for the right mixture of energy, spirit and creativity that you bring to the table. Don't let anyone talk you out

attracted to me because of my commitment to open a store selling chocolate chip cookies. The first was Roland Young, who was creative director at A&M Records. One day I was passing out cookies in his office, as I did from time to time, and as I started to leave his office I turned and yelled, "Roland, I'm going to open a store selling chocolate chip cookies." He called back, "Outta sight, let me do the graphics." I didn't even know I *needed* graphics and here was a guy volunteering to do them for me.

The second was Tony Christian, a very talented artist friend and neighbor. Tony was visiting one day while I was experimenting with chocolate chip cookies made with peanut butter. I served Tony a few samples, with milk, on my best plate and he got so excited he decided he just had to design some furniture for my store. Not only did he design three tables, a counter and a pedestal for the mixing bowl I had used at home, but he also shingled the eating area, laid the solid oak tile floor and with his lady friend, Norma, arranged plants inside and out. I do not believe Roland and Tony would have responded so enthusiastically had I told them, "I'm gonna *try* to open a store," "I *guess* I'll open a store," or "I *hope* I can open a store." In each instance with the strength of commitment I said to them, "I am going to open a store selling chocolate chip cookies."

82   It was my *commitment* that attracted Roland and Tony into my life, and it was also my commitment that got them involved. Commitment is truly the great activator of the universe. When you say unequivocally "I will," it sets off a chain reaction that begins sending you whatever or whoever it is you need to help you successfully complete your goal. Commitment also creates opportunities for others to express themselves.

One way I've discovered to strengthen my commitment is by living in the present, by keeping all areas of my life as current as possible. Don't put off anything until tomorrow. I believe that *one today* truly is worth *two tomorrows.*

I decided the beginning of 1987 would be different for me. I wanted to be more focused, more organized, and I made a commitment to do just that. I went on a fourteen-day cleansing fast. Fasting always helps to center me spiritually and get my thoughts together. To help keep me on top of things in my office I decided to take the advice once read in a magazine article, "never touch the same piece of paper twice." Let me tell you, it really works. I even took the concept further by never touching the same plate or glass twice. Never touching the same shirt or pair of pants twice after taking them off. You'd be surprised how clean your house becomes when you do that and how much free time you have as a result of living in the present. Doing it now never allows things to accumulate. When someone asked W. Clement what was the most important advice he could give, he replied; Do it! Do it! Do it!

Making a commitment is one of the best ways to get your life back on track and the residual effects in other areas of your life are extremely rewarding. I can honestly report that 1987 started off better than any previous year and was directly related to the commitment I made at the beginning of the year.

How many times have you said to yourself, "I'll start when I get enough money; when I meet the right partner; when the time is right, etc. etc."? The best time to start anything is when you get the idea, and the degree to which you succeed is directly related to the strength of your commitment. That's what I did with creating Famous Amos. I got the idea to open a store selling chocolate chip cookies. I made a definite commitment to do just that, and the strength of my commitment took me through the entire process one step at a time. Some people said the economic times were not right, with sugar and flour being priced at an all-time high. Others said in order to open a bakery you needed twenty-nine or thirty different items. Others said the location I had chosen was a bad location. Just about everyone I talked with about opening a store selling chocolate chip cookies had a reason why it would not work. If I had listened to any one of them I never would have sold my first cookie. Instead, I made a commitment to open one store selling chocolate chip cookies; I didn't let anything take me away from that commitment; and I succeeded.

In seeking a way to become more committed, it might be helpful to remember Goethe's words, "Boldness has genius, power and magic in it. Only engage and the mind grows heated, begin and then the task will be completed." If there is one truth I've learned it is this, "you will never complete anything you start unless you first begin." The fastest runner in the world will never cross the finish line unless he or she first *begins* the race. The great inventions of the world never would have occurred unless the inventor made the *first step*. If you really want to change your life, count the number of times you've said, "I will," then count the number of times you've said, "I can't." If you're not where you want to be, chances are you've said, "I can't" more times than you've said, "I will." Taking that first step involves "I will," and "I will" is the beginning of commitment. It's a BIG STEP. The first step is *always* a BIG STEP. But it promises a BIG reward. You get to keep the reward *plus* you have the satisfaction of knowing you earned it yourself.

> Not only does commitment bring you rewards and satisfaction, it also produces achievement and fun.

Oftentimes it takes the personal experience of someone making a commitment to *you* that inspires you to make a commitment to someone or something else. This was the case with Bill Milliken. Bill was a kid who spent far more time out of school than he did in school until a caring adult came to his hangout at a local pool hall, took an interest in him and made a commitment to support him in turning his life around. That act of love left a lasting impression on young Bill and years later he committed his life to the youth of our country as one of the founders of The Street Academy, which later turned into Cities-In-Schools, now a national organization dedicated to helping young people continue their schooling and learning how to feel good about who they are.

As a board member of Cities-In-Schools who

has worked first hand with Bill and the other members who started this very worthwhile program, I can attest to the fact that their commitment made in the 1960s is stronger today than ever before. I am constantly inspired and strengthened by the depth of their commitment and dedication. It is truly a blessing for me to be associated with them for I have gotten new insight into the meaning of the word "commitment." From this example you can see how making a commitment is comparable to throwing a pebble in a lake. The ripples roll on to touch the lives of many for years into the future.

This is just one story of many I've encountered that inspired me to further strengthen my commitment. There have also been many people who have reached into my life and made a commitment to me. One who immediately comes to mind is Sadie Brown who owned the secretarial school I attended when I returned home to New York City, after being discharged from the Air Force in 1957. Mrs. Brown not only made a commitment to me, she made a commitment to all the students who proved to her that they were willing to make a commitment to themselves. As long as you kept your part of that bargain, she would keep hers. That also showed me commitment began and ended with me.

We all have those teachers and supporters in

our lives whose examples we can review from time to time to help strengthen and renew our commit-ment.

Commitment in Relationships

Have you examined your commitment to your relationship recently? Have you even *made* a com-mitment to your relationship? Many times it's easy to make a commitment to achieving a material goal or to your job, but extremely difficult to make a commitment to a personal relationship. For many of us, that's the most difficult hurdle to overcome.

For years I had been great at committing myself to work or the pursuit of material gain. But when it came to making a commitment to a relationship, I always fell short of the mark. Finally, after two failed marriages and many aborted relationships, I realized that Christine, a woman I had lived with for almost two years but had separated from because I was not prepared to make a commitment, really loved me. It was the first time I had acknowledged the love of a mate. I recognized this as a sign of growth.

I decided to stop running from relationships and commit myself to making this one work. We made our vows on a beautiful Hawaiian day—July 1, 1979. Because of a commitment I made and kept, my life has been more joyful and meaningful than ever before. It has required a lot of work from both of us, but because of our mutual commitment, we have been able to contribute whatever was necessary to strengthen our relationship.

In order for you to make a commitment to someone or something, you must believe in what or who it is. This creates an excitement and an enthusiasm for the commitment. It is also important to believe in yourself. Edgar A. Guest wrote a poem entitled, "It Couldn't Be Done," that speaks directly to the subject of commitment. This could be the entrepreneur's creed:

> Somebody said that it couldn't be done
> But he with a chuckle replied
> That maybe it couldn't, but he would be one
> Who wouldn't say so till he'd tried
> So he buckled right in with the trace of a grin
> On his face. If he worried he hid it.
> He started to sing as he tackled the thing
> That couldn't be done, and he did it.
>
> Somebody scoffed: "Oh, you'll never do that;
> At least no one has ever done it";
> But he took off his coat and he took off his hat,
> And the first thing we knew he'd begun it.
> With a lift of his chin and a bit of a grin
> Without any doubting or quiddit

THE POWER IN COMMITMENT

He started to sing as he tackled the thing
That couldn't be done, and he did it.

There are thousands to tell you it cannot be done,
There are thousands to prophesy failure
There are thousands to point out to you, one by one,
The dangers that wait to assail you.
But just buckle right in with a bit of a grin.
Just take off your coat and go to it;
Just start to sing as you tackle the thing
That "cannot be done," and you'll do it.

Whenever I read that poem I always think of "The Little Engine That Could." The Little Engine made a commitment to carry the train over the mountain and believing in his heart of hearts that he could repeated, over and over as he inched his way up the mountain, "I think I can, I think I can," until he was almost to the top. Then he began to shout, "I know I can, I know I can." It was his belief that made him take on the job, coupled with the strength of his commitment that got him to the top of the mountain.

It doesn't matter how many people say it cannot be done or how many people have tried it before, it's important to realize that whatever you're doing, it's your first attempt at it.

90   You're a unique individual with a different energy, a different spirit and creative ideas. You bring something to everything you do that no one else has, and if you add a strong commitment to that, it might be just the ingredient to take you over the mountain.

It might also help to remember that surely someone said to Henry Ford, "Henry, you can't build a motor car. Why it'll scare all the horses away. You're just wasting your time." And I'll bet there were many who told Thomas Edison his idea of the light bulb was ludicrous. How many times do you think Benjamin Franklin was told, "Franklin there's absolutely no connection between lightning and electricity." In my own case, just about everyone said to me, "Wally, you'll never be successful opening a store selling only chocolate chip cookies."

At times like these, it might be helpful to recall Goethe's words, "Are you in earnest?" Do you really want to achieve this task you are undertaking? Do you have that burning desire to see it completed? Can you really taste it? If the answer to these questions is "yes" then you are ready to heed the next bit of advice that Goethe gives, "Seek this very minute, whatever you can do, or dream you can, begin it." He couldn't be more candid. He says nothing about having enough money, waiting for the right time. He says, "Seek this very minute."

That means starting right where you are. Goethe urges, "Whatever you can do, or dream you can, begin it."

Commitment or procrastination? Which path will you take? Are you ready to take off your coat and hat and begin? Are you ready to move forward with your chin held high with "a bit of a grin," without any "doubting or quiddit"? Are you ready to make a commitment to tackling the thing that everyone says cannot be done? If you are ready to take these positive steps, then you are ready to have your deepest dreams fulfilled.

"Commitment" is truly one of the most powerful words in the English language. It can bring magic and instant gratification in your life.

If I have any secrets, tapping into the power of commitment must be one of them. Make a commitment right now to exercise your power in commitment. If I can do it so can you.

5

THE POWER IN INTEGRITY

Let there be a new high standard of honesty, industry and integrity in our society, and let it begin with ME!

Have you noticed that these seem to be the times of "Do anything you want to do, as long as you don't get caught"? And have you noticed, these also seem to be the times of deep-seated scandal in all areas of our society, because those people who operate with this type of me-over-everybody-else belief always get caught when they go too far? They always get caught because they always go too far. A person's actions *should not* be dictated by how much that person thinks he or she can get away with. Perhaps a rationale is that, to some people society says: "I dare you, see if you can get away with it." That lure may or may not exist. But what I'm going to examine in this chapter is personal integrity.

When I run into past associates, acquaintances or old buddies, I do not have to bow my head or look away in an attempt to prevent them from seeing me. That's an aspect of my life that I am really proud of. I like to think that I can look people, no matter what relationship I had with them, square in the eyes because I've lived my life with a large degree of integrity. A person's actions should not be prescribed by society or institutions because these structures can never allow for every situation. A gap or loophole can always be found. A person's actions should be prescribed by his or her own morals.

> Morality, integrity and ethics are the foundation on which one builds one's life.

Integrity plays a part in every area of your life, in both business and personal relationships. Whenever and wherever you come into contact with people, you will be calling upon your personal code of ethics.

Some think that integrity and moral standards are values dictated by our governments, corporations, and educational institutions, the institutions that more often than not set the trends and directions that our nation follows. Let's examine this concept further. Governments are institutions created to represent and enforce the will of the individual people that form them. Corporations exist to provide a product or service that fills some need created by people. Educational facilities help expand the young minds of our society. In many instances those directions come as inspiration from the path of a great mind that has gone before. In every case, people are the bottom line. Governments, educational institutions and corporations all exist to serve people. When we take a sideline position and let the structures we've created run by themselves, we're bound to end up someplace we hadn't expected to go.

Integrity, like everything else in our world, begins with the individual and extends outward into all of the institutions we create. But at its most basic level, integrity is highly personal and individual. Emerson referred to "The sacredness of private integrity." Those people whose actions have been publicly judged as morally wrong may be publicly criticized and then even ostracized. But in the end, after the scandal has been forgotten, those people are left to face themselves for the final judgment on their deeds.

What Integrity Is

I often speak on college campuses and many times I find that the students are led to believe one set of ethics and integrity exist for business and another set for personal life. This is probably one of the first areas where we begin to let go of responsibility for our own integrity. Searching through the dictionary I have found "ethics" and "integrity" to be listed only once. That leads me to believe that those definitions should apply to the ethics and integrity in all areas of your life. "Ethics" is defined as, "The study of the general nature of morals and of the specific moral choices to be made by the *individual* in his relationship with others." Notice, the definition reads: "in his *relationship* with others." It doesn't say that ethics can be used or ignored depending on the situations or circumstances. The definition also talks about the general nature of morals and of the *choices* to be made. The definition covers all areas of life and establishes that a choice

is involved. The last important aspect of the definition says: "by the *individual*." The individual remains
responsible for his or her ethics and always with a
choice.

"Integrity" is defined as the "rigid adherence to
a code of behavior." I would like to add the word
"positive" before "behavior" so that the definition
would read: "the rigid adherence to a code of positive behavior." I add positive because the key to
tapping into the power of integrity lies in affirming
only the positive attributes of one's moral standards.
There is no distinction made between business and
personal ethics or business and personal integrity.
Yet, I can understand how one might operate under
dual standards. Once I lived my life believing in one
set of rules for my business life and another set for
my personal life.

To have integrity one must be honest. I was not
honest in my relationships with my first two wives. I
used all of the typical excuses; hard work for my
family and their security was the justification for not
spending time at home. Believe me, I did work hard.
However, much of the time I spent away from home
was not necessarily spent on office work. The mind
can and will find any way to justify doing what we
tell it to do. That is a most fascinating aspect of
ourselves: our mind is always at work, whether we

use it positively or negatively. In my mind I attempted to fool myself into believing what I did was right and good. Reflecting on that time in my life, when I lacked integrity, I realize now how unhappy I made myself, and those closest to me. In looking for ways to justify my behavior, I had split into two different people operating in two different worlds. I have found that the times when I was short on integrity I was also trying to be dishonest with myself. I say "trying," because the truth of the matter is, you can never lie to yourself. Somewhere inside you always know that you're not telling the truth.

There came a time when I outgrew the game. I began to need more substance in my behavior. That was my psyche's way of calling for some integrity to be added to my life. I began, with tremendous success, to be truthful with myself first. I stopped lying to myself. As a result, my actions began to correspond with my thoughts. In the process I am sure I stopped confusing people by saying one thing and then doing another. As I began to develop a habit of being truthful, I began to extend that truth to those who entered my life. The process has not been easy and is by no means complete; while many years have passed, I seem to have traveled only a short distance. I do not want to give the impression that I changed 180 degrees overnight. A lot of these changes are like skills that must be practiced and practiced, until one day after you've forgotten all of the time invested, you notice that you're pretty good at what you're doing. That's why patience is so important. I feel that I have made progress and that progress can be measured by the improved quality of my life. I am now at peace with myself; I was not before.

Peace of mind is what integrity means to me. Integrity is internal. Society cannot inflict it on us. The quality of our lives is a direct result of the measure of our integrity. And it's a rock-solid principle available to all those who wish to put it to the test.

I am reminded of some stories of other individuals and their integrity. We can all be strengthened and motivated by the personal and individual situations in the lives of others. Do you view stories about people and how they've changed as good news? You should, because they are reminders that you can always change the conditions of your life, if you want to. With integrity as one of the major building blocks for a meaningful and fulfilled life, you can be comforted by the fact that you personally control your switches. If something is going wrong in your life, you know to rely on these principles

100 and look within at your attitude for the corrections needed to get you going on the right track again. You also must look outside, at the physical manifestations in your life as markers by which you can judge the correctness of your integrity. We produce whatever exists in our lives with our minds. If you do not get positive results from your actions, you know that something within you needs adjusting.

When I look for my role models of uncompromising integrity, the first to immediately come to mind is my mother, Ruby.

During the days of segregation in the South, when maintaining self-respect and integrity for Black people proved as difficult a task as everyday survival, my mother worked as a domestic. She showed tremendous integrity in her work. She demanded, and received, a decent wage. Her work was of the highest quality, so she always had more work than she could handle, and on her own terms. She taught me to always do your very best, and to have a sense of pride in every area of your life.

Even beyond her job, my mother stood firm behind her beliefs. She still stands firm today. For me, Ruby's finest hour occurred one Sunday in 1944, on a bus in our home town, Tallahassee, Florida. The South, 1944: it was a segregated bus. Whites in the front, Blacks in the rear. On this particular day,

Ruby decided to sit in the front of the bus. It was practically empty, except for a young white woman, whom we later discovered was the bus driver's girl-friend. My mother decided to sit next to this lady. Ruby felt justified in her action because we had done a lot of walking and she said her feet were hurting. Almost immediately, the lady complained to the bus driver. He turned to Ruby and told her to move to the rear of the bus. The conflict came from the fact that very few people ever told my mother what to do. "I paid my money and I'm gonna sit where I please," was Ruby's proud response to the bus driver. This was not acceptable behavior; I anticipated trouble. The driver didn't know exactly what to do. I suppose he had not expected such a defiant re-sponse from a Black woman. He drove on for the time being. But as soon as we reached one of the depots on the route, he went inside to get some advice or help in handling this adamant woman. He returned alone and once again demanded that Ruby move to the rear of the bus. Once again, Ruby stoutly refused. The standoff: should the driver phys-ically move my mother to the rear of the bus (which probably would have been an impossible task because of Ruby's strength and determination); or should he move on about his business of driving the bus? After looking over the other passengers who had since

102 boarded, he decided to concede this battle and return to his route. His decision probably hinged on the fact that the other passengers who had boarded were all young, Black servicemen. They had been sitting quietly waiting for the driver's next move.

Although I was frightened out of my wits, I felt proud of my mother that day; and through the years as I've gained more knowledge, I've developed more respect for the courage Ruby displayed in maintaining her dignity and her integrity. I recalled my mother's courage ten years later when Rosa Parks decided to "sit" for her dignity and integrity by refusing to give up her seat to a white passenger in Montgomery, Alabama. That decision not to compromise her personal integrity triggered the well-known bus boycott led by Dr. Martin Luther King, Jr. In addition, that individual decision sparked a movement that changed the moral stature of an entire nation. I've often thought, had events gone another way that day in Tallahassee, Ruby would have been the first Amos to be famous.

There are other examples of what integrity means when translated into physical, results-of-your-life terms. I read a story of a family who sold their business. The buyer never conducted an audit (the books had never been audited!), never took an inventory, verified receivables or checked property titles. The buyer turned over a check for fifty-five million dollars on that family's word. Now that's unheard of in business. But it happened because a family made every area of their lives an extension of their personal honesty. There are great rewards in knowing that you conduct your life in a manner that raises the standards of our society. Although our actions begin with us as individuals, they spread out into the world and influence others in an ever growing circle. We are all role models. Our goal is to be a *positive* role model.

I read another story about a businessman who closed deals not with a lengthy legal contract, but with a simple handshake. He reasoned that his clients gave him their confidence; with that he had an obligation to uphold his company's reputation.

I've dealt with my own company in very much the same way. I think of Famous Amos as an extension of myself. My early days of exposure to a person with great integrity (my mother) laid the foundation for developing integrity in my life. I've always thought that a job completed by me bears my signature or trademark. It holds a portion of my personal identity. I've carried this belief with me since my entry into the workplace as a shoe shine boy many years ago in Tallahassee. I've infused that integrity into Famous Amos. The company represents everything I've become. I found a quote that says it far more beautifully than I ever could: "If a task is once begun, never leave it till it's done. Be the labor great or small, do it well, or not at all." These ethics do not permit the double standard of one set for business and another set for personal use.

Integrity is demonstrated in two distinct areas of The Famous Amos Chocolate Chip Cookie Company. One is in the product. We have consistently maintained a high level of quality in our ingredients, packaging and over-all presentation. We have also maintained the percentage of ingredients. I am always leery of products claiming a twenty to forty percent increase in their main ingredients as a public relations move to make us think they are improving on our behalf. The real reason is probably low sales and they need a gimmick to get us to buy. Why can't those products start out with the higher amount of ingredients? A forty percent increase of something scarce to begin with is not much of an improvement. A product cannot gain integrity by being dubious about the quality or quantity of its ingredients.

The second area that Famous Amos has maintained a high degree of integrity in is the image I convey to the public. I have always been consistent in what I've thought, said, and done. What I present to the public as Famous Amos, the man, is Wally Amos. We are the same person; one is not a character nor a facade. I've always maintained my actions as an extension of my belief system. My goal has been not only excellence in product, but moral excellence as well. I wanted to build a company with sound principles and high ideals.

The last case history on individual integrity, and probably the most dynamic is that of one human being whose name rings synonymous with integrity: Buckminster Fuller. Fuller actually lived his life as an experiment in discovering the difference an individual can make that great corporations, nations and religions cannot. He proved that an individual can make a difference and still maintain his integrity. He was an inventor, a writer and a thinker. Some of his inventions include the World Game, the Dymaxion Airocean World Map, his development of Synergetic Geometry and his most famous invention, the Geodesic Dome. I was stationed at Hickam Air Force Base, in Honolulu, Hawaii, when his first dome was constructed. They said it would collapse. They were wrong, it's still standing. Years later, I had the pleasure and benefit of Buckminster Fuller's genius by taping my television show, The Wally Amos Happiness Show, in that same dome. Fuller wrote twenty-four books and gave lectures and

106   workshops, sharing his theories with people around the world. He did all of this after reversing his life from being an alcoholic at the point of suicide. Imagine that! How many social programs that strive to combat alcoholism, depression or any other disease can boast of such a complete and successful cure in any of their patients?

Buckminster Fuller's accomplishments represent just a sampling of the potential of the human being who lives a life based on the empowering principles of integrity. He also proved that integrity allows you to think with extreme clarity and to extend love to all other "Earthians," as he often referred to humans. Bucky, as he was affectionately called by many, gave true meaning to the quote, "Let there be a new high standard of honesty, industry and integrity in our society, and let it begin with me."

Juxtapose his life and accomplishments against the lives led by individuals who permit their integrity to be molded and manipulated externally. Buckminster Fuller, a man of moral stature, set trends rather than be defined by them. How much stronger would our society—our world society, unencumbered by boundaries that make us think we are separate—be if more individuals followed Bucky's example of setting the pace?

The Bible suggests that we become "as little children." It occurs to me that children have a tremendous integrity. They tell you exactly what's on their minds.

> Work on developing that wonderful childlike quality of integrity within you.

As you journey through life, adopt the following as your personal affirmation, repeating it often so that it may become a part of your every action: "Let there be a new high standard of honesty, industry and integrity in our society, and let it begin with ME!"

6

THE POWER IN GIVING

To give and to receive are one in truth

Some people live life as if it were a horizontal line with all of us standing in it single file, fighting desperately to get to the front of the line. Fearing there isn't enough to go around, they will do whatever possible to get to the front of the line—steal, lie, even kill. My experiences in giving have helped me to see that life is a circle with enough to go around for everybody. We are all standing in that circle holding hands, and what you give to the circle comes back to you.

110   When you give love and peace to the circle you receive love and peace in return. When you give hate you get hate. And when you give money and prosperity, you get money and prosperity in return. So you want to be careful what you give to the circle because as the saying goes, "What goes around comes around." The world is not as big as many of us would like to believe, and you really do get what you give. Giving is always receiving.

What is your definition of giving? Have you ever thought about the spiritual aspect of giving, or do you constantly focus on the physical or material realm? I realize that sometimes it's difficult to understand spiritual giving because we are so conditioned to think of material giving, usually in terms of money. We are often concerned with *getting* money, and once we've gotten it we don't want to let it go. But there comes a time for most of us when we begin to see that giving spiritually is more than giving materially. Some of the most meaningful experiences I have had were the times I gave of myself to help someone. There is a poem entitled "Miracles," written by Winifred Brand, herself a most giving and gentle lady, that sums up the idea of giving:

All of us work miracles, sometime, somewhere, somehow; it could be one is possible for you to work right now. A smile for one who's weary, a hand to one alone, a word of hope and courage, where caring is unknown. I didn't feed a multitude, command the wind or rain, change water into wine or make the blind to see again, but I have brought a smile of peace where brows were knit with care, and I have brought a touch of love where hate was everywhere. And if you look on such as these that life and faith renew, why they are little miracles that anyone can do.

If you had known me as a youngster you would have thought that King Midas was my hero. Everyone knows the story of King Midas, who made everything he touched turn to gold. Well, as a youngster I had a reputation for holding on to whatever was mine. Rumor had it that I was even quite stingy. That unsharing attitude followed me into adulthood! Well, King Midas got his wish but soon discovered he couldn't rest on a solid gold mattress or kiss a human being who he had turned to gold. He learned the hard way—as many of us do—that true wealth isn't great quantities of gold or silver. True wealth is peace of mind gained from living a life of service. Part of what we fail to understand is that the true essence of giving is that we receive in direct proportion to what we have given.

There is a place called St. Elmo Village, which

112   embodies this spirit of giving and was one of my first
learning experiences in true giving. Several years
before I was Famous Amos—B.C. (Before Cookie),
when I was Wally Amos, private citizen—I got
involved in a neighborhood improvement project
located in the southwest area of Los Angeles. I was
so deeply touched by the effort, love and humanity
that permeated the area, I just had to become a part
of it. St. Elmo Village is like that; it's spirit just
draws you.

My first visit there was to attend a fundraiser.
There was a two-story apartment complex to the
right of St. Elmo, with another housing development across the street. Directly across the street
from St. Elmo was a boarded-up vacant house with
weeds and brown grass in its front yard. As I drove
up, all I could see were these buildings. The neighborhood was really deteriorating, on its way to becoming a ghetto. But stuck in the middle of this
urban desert was the oasis of St. Elmo Village. The
driveway, a "U" through the back of the property,
had been transformed into a beautiful, brightly
painted mural. The village was a collection of small
houses surrounded by painted sidewalks and muraled
fences, with sculptures in the front yards and smil-
ing, friendly people everywhere. On this night,

dinners were being sold for two dollars each to raise money for the down payment to buy the property on which those homes stood.

A warm, friendly sensation came over me as I entered the room where the meeting was being held. The walls were covered with artwork created by Rozzell Sykes and his nephew Roderick. They spearheaded the group, which operated under the premise that even though you might live in a shoe box, it didn't have to look like a shoe box. They converted everything into art. They even turned the bathtub into a piece of art by painting a naked lady in the bottom. It was their way of giving life to everything and making it useful. They painted everything and anything—I began to think that if I didn't move around, they might paint me! They were encouraging people to use whatever resources they have to beautify their world. Rozzell once said to me: "Whatever you have can always be better than it is. You don't have to settle for what is; it is up to each individual to make their life the very best." At that meeting on my first visit to St. Elmo, we were applying that philosophy by saving the cluster of ten houses that comprised St. Elmo Village from becoming the site of another one of those impersonal, sterile apartment buildings. I say "we" because from my first time there, I could tell that I had come to a very special place, and their cause would become my cause.

Ultimately, we were able to raise the fifteen thousand dollars needed for the down payment. I helped by using my show business contacts to give St. Elmo some exposure in the local media. I even had a joint birthday party there with a friend, Sam Denoff, whose birthday is the same day as mine. Instead of receiving gifts, he and I suggested donations be made to the village. Not only was I receiving gratification from being associated with St. Elmo and working with them, but I was learning from a front row seat what real giving was all about.

St. Elmo Village gives back everything it receives. All of the materials used went toward rehabilitating the dilapidated houses and beautifying the community. The human energy expended is returned in the form of community pride and increased self-worth through investments of time and effort. St. Elmo Village is still there, a community always giving back what it has received by teaching people how to live, create and make a difference through art and imagination. Those of us who did not live there, but gave time, energy and material possessions, benefitted from those ideals as much as anybody else. St. Elmo Village, a channel through which Rozzell and Roderick Sykes worked and expressed themselves, was also a lesson in love for me and offered insight into what my own potential was.

Rozzell visited me shortly before Christmas, 1974, when I was trying to raise money to open my first cookie store and also borrow money for Christmas gifts. He slipped fifty dollars into my hands, which represented half of all the money he had in the world. That is the spirit of giving. Living your life in that spirit can only make you grow.

> Lead a life of service to your fellow human beings, giving your all to that purpose, and you will have nothing else in life to worry about.

I like to refer to charitable causes as "vehicles for giving." A "vehicle for giving" is a situation created to offer an individual the opportunity to serve and give, either monetarily or by the giving of his or her time or services. In return, the individual experiences the joy of giving, plus receives the love and support of all those participating in that particular vehicle for giving.

What is your definition of charity? To some, the concept of charity has been perverted to mean a free ride. While it is true that we must always help each other by sharing, we must also understand that nothing is free. In our travels we all come across people begging for money. In many instances, they have no apparent handicaps, and we may wonder what keeps them from working and *giving* themselves.

I do not suggest that you *not* give in these situations, because I am not here to judge. To be in tune with the spirit of giving means that you give without expecting to receive in return. What I want to express is that we *all* must contribute to the circle. If we all lead lives of service, then we all take care of each other. However, in addition to our responsibility to the person next to us in the circle, we each have a responsibility to ourselves. There are people who are looking for a free ride when such a thing does not exist. Is it possible that the person seeking a handout is not being helped by receiving it? Can a person be made dependent on some outside means of support not because they *can't* take responsibility for themselves, but because they *won't*? In some instances, this is what charity has become.

The price paid for supporting the individual who has abdicated his or her responsibility to themselves is the price of an increased strain placed upon the circle. The circle becomes weaker because one of the links has become weaker. Do you wish to continue giving to someone or something that does nothing but take and take while never giving in return? Giving is a win-win situation; taking is a lose-lose drain.

Part of our responsibility as human beings is to find vehicles for giving that allow for win-win situations—like St. Elmo Village. However, we must be cautious not to give blindly to ideals that can hurt us all.

Another win-win vehicle I had the pleasure to climb aboard was the Hollypark Library in Hawthorne, California, channeled through Dennis Martin, the head librarian, and a most dedicated human being. I first met Dennis and the Hollypark community children when I went by to share some cookies and autograph posters during Black History Week.

The children's enthusiastic reception of me gave Dennis the idea of Famous Amos sponsoring a reading challenge for the kids, with chocolate chip cookies as the reward. I was honored that Dennis thought the children would want my cookies badly enough to read. And I liked the idea of my cookies being the sweetener to what many children consider a bitter chore: improving their reading skills.

It was a three-month program at Hollypark

118   Library and every child who read eight books in a two-week period and wrote a report on the books would receive a one-pound bag of cookies as a reward.

I am happy to say the program was an overwhelming success. Famous Amos gladly gave away fifteen hundred, one-pound bags of cookies to the young readers who qualified.

Giving to the Hollypark Library was, in my estimation, some of the most meaningful giving I could perform. Encouraging young people to read is one of the best investments in the future one can possibly make. Reading is the foundation for education and knowledge, and education and knowledge form the foundation of one's well-being.

Hollypark provided me with the opportunity to witness, first hand, another dedicated, giving human being. Dennis Martin was a positive role model of the first order because he demonstrated the attribute of giving, *going the extra mile*. But more than that, Dennis Martin enhanced my life. Once again, I received blessings in abundance because I dared to give.

I strongly believe the success I've enjoyed in the cookie business is directly related to the giving I've shared with others. Being famous simply means people recognize you. I feel there's no real value in being a celebrity unless that celebrity or fame can be used to help others. (I came across a definition of celebrity that says, "celebrity is the art of being known by those who do not know you.") From the moment I became Famous Amos, I knew that one day I would lend my name, fame and reputation to help bring awareness to a national cause. Throughout my life many people have helped me and I saw Famous Amos as my opportunity to give something back to the circle. I didn't know it at the time but my involvement with the Hollypark Library was preparing me for an opportunity to give in a very big way.

In 1978, my friend and business associate, John Rosica, told me about a friend of his who tutored adult non-readers for an organization called Literacy Volunteers of America. L.V.A. was formed in 1962, by Ruth Colvin, in an attempt to help the many adults in her community who could not read and write. Later, Mrs. Colvin expanded on her idea by working with professional reading consultants to develop a training method for non-professional volunteers to teach basic reading and writing to adults and teenagers. The method was successful, and L.V.A. spread to other states and communities.

John suggested that this might be the cause we had been looking for. He went on to explain that

120 there were twenty-three million native-born, adult Americans who could neither read nor write. These millions were called "functional illiterates." The phrase means that they read below a fifth grade level. I was stunned to hear such shocking news. I had never considered illiteracy as a problem: this is America, one of the richest countries in the world. Surely we can all read. Well we can't. And worse yet, I was not the only person who took it for granted that everyone could read and write. After talking with John, I knew immediately that we had found our national vehicle for giving. Here was a problem that affected a vast majority of our citizens in all walks of life—all races, religions and colors. It was exactly the type of vehicle I sought. I wanted to be able to serve a wide cross-section, as many people as possible.

Johnny (sometimes I call him Johnny) and I visited L.V.A. headquarters in Syracuse, New York, to meet with the executive board and Ruth Colvin, to ask if I could serve as their national spokesperson.

Even though they were considered a national organization, most of their programs were concentrated in the northeast. I offered to change that by giving them national exposure which would help them to spread their program throughout the United States. At first, they were a little suspicious of my

THE POWER IN GIVING

intentions. (Promoters don't have the best images.)
I made it clear to them I would not stop selling
cookies during my promotional tours, but I would be
selling L.V.A. in addition to cookies. I also pointed
out to them that I would continue to promote
cookies whether I worked with L.V.A. or not, however no one was currently conveying L.V.A.'s message to the people. I made the commitment to raise
money, get new tutors and work to give L.V.A.
greater national exposure, all at no cost to L.V.A.
Talk about a deal you can't refuse!

Shortly after, they accepted my offer. I went to
Syracuse to learn first-hand exactly what Literacy
Volunteers of America was all about and the meth-
ods used to teach adults to read and write. It was
not my intention to be a figurehead. I wanted to
know the inner workings of the organization so that
as their spokesperson I could represent them accurately and with enthusiasm. Through experience, I
have discovered that my level of enthusiasm goes up
proportionately to my knowledge of the subject matter. I confirmed the degree of my commitment by
going to Syracuse in February for my indoctrina-
tion—*nobody* willingly goes to Syracuse in February!

On April 10, 1979, I was officially introduced
at a news conference held at the Lincoln Center
Library in New York City, as the national spokesper-

122 son for Literacy Volunteers of America. Since then all the suspicions about my intentions have disappeared. I have criss-crossed the United States taking the message of L.V.A. to millions of people. In the process, not only have I achieved my main goal of raising the level of awareness regarding the problems of illiteracy in America, but I have recruited many hundreds of students and tutors, helped raise many thousands of dollars, and even donated my own funds.

Being involved with L.V.A. has allowed me to fulfill what I have come to consider my sole purpose for existing: serving my fellow human beings. Meeting the students and tutors involved with the program has been among the most gratifying and rewarding experiences of my life, and has proven to me conclusively that giving and receiving are one. When you give, you get and in kind. Not only have I received warmth, love and great inner gratification as a result of my involvement with Literacy Volunteers, but it has also helped my business. It truly has been a win-win situation. And once again, I have encountered another incredibly giving human being, Ruth Colvin. I am absolutely overwhelmed at the depth of her giving. She has taken a social statistic that is virtually incomprehensible in human terms and has done just that: she has made it humanly understandable. She has defined a statistic of twenty-seven million functionally illiterate adults as *one person teaching another person to read*. With her giving, selfless attitude Ruth Colvin started a one-on-one tutorial program, multiplied by thousands, making a difference to the individual involved and also "chipping away" at that staggering number of twenty-seven million. Isn't it incredible how giving works?

When you give to the enormous circle that is our world, your gift multiplies and has an effect, not only on the individuals directly involved, but throughout the entire universe. The spirit of giving is strengthened immensely by you giving your gift.

When I was visiting Minneapolis, doing some work with the Minnesota Literacy Council, I was given a reading entitled "Starfish," as a thank you. It not only changed my attitude about my contributions to the campaign for literacy, but it gave me new insight into how I can make a difference in the lives of all my fellow men and women, boys and

124   girls. As you read this piece, read with your *heart* as well as with your eyes.

> As the old man walked down a Spanish beach at dawn, he saw ahead of him what he thought to be a dancer. The young man was running across the sand rhythmically bending down to pick up a stranded starfish and throw it far into the sea. The old man gazed in wonder as the young soul again and again threw the small starfish from the sand to the water. The old man approached him and asked why he spent so much energy doing what seemed a waste of time. The young man explained that the stranded starfish would die if left until the morning sun.
>
> "But there must be thousands of miles of beach and millions of starfish. How can your effort make any difference?"
>
> The young man looked down at the small starfish in his hand and as he threw it to safety in the sea said, "It makes a difference to this one."

Isn't that a powerful writing? The simplest thing always seems to be the most profound.

If you can help just one person, as Ruth Colvin did, you would have made a difference to that person and to yourself. If we all help just one person, think of the powerful difference in the world we could accomplish.

Emerson said, "Every business is the extended shadow of one man," and I would add, one woman.

Every vehicle for giving is the extended shadow of one man or woman. It all starts with *you*.

Giving More

I don't consider this a "how-to" book but here are a few ways I have discovered to help me increase my giving consciousness. The benefit for me has been tremendous growth in my personal and business life.

One way I increase my giving consciousness is to *always give more than I am asked* to give—going that extra mile. So often we are called upon to perform and we give just enough to get by. If we continue to give only enough to get by we will be creating a life of mediocrity, a life "that's good enough." By holding back you can never have an opportunity to experience excellence and all of the joy and rewards that life has in store for you. Everything you associate yourself with will be mediocre because that is the type of energy and spirit you will have created.

Another method I use is to *give before I'm asked.* If I'm working and see something that needs to be done, I do it, even if it isn't my job. We're all employees of the same company working for the same goals, working in the same circle.

> When I can give more than is asked of me, before it is asked of me, it enhances the whole company, my worth to the company, and my worth as an individual. Remember, never let the words, "it's not my job" pass your lips.

When I'm walking and see a piece of paper in my path, I'll pick it up rather than walk over it. I want to live in a litter-free environment, so I give to that ideal by helping to pick up litter. Just think, if we all picked up litter when we had the opportunity, we would live in a litter-free world. Today, take a chance and start giving before you're asked and watch the conditions of your world improve.

A great test for me to tell if I should give to a certain situation or not is to ask myself, "Can I afford to do this?" If I start coming up with reasons why I can't give, it's a definite sign that I really need to give—and right now. If you think you can't afford to, that really is a sure sign that you can't afford not to give.

I once got a request for the company to make a donation to help a group of wheelchair youngsters participate in a sporting event. We were having severe cash flow problems and my first reaction was,

"We can't afford to. Why, we don't even have enough money to pay our vendors." Then I thought, surely one hundred dollars to these children won't be the straw to break the camel's back. And it wasn't. We helped the children and continued to do business—with a stronger consciousness.

Reverend Ike has a great analogy. He says, "for the man with one hundred pairs of shoes to give you a pair of shoes is no big deal. But for the man who has only one pair of shoes to give you his only pair is real selfless giving."

The next time you can't afford to give, can't afford the time to volunteer, to spend time with your family, or can't afford to make a donation, give anyway and observe how fantastic you feel afterwards. We all have a lot to give, and every time we give our supply is replenished. Giving and receiving is one in truth.

To some, these ideas might seem abstract. But believe me when I say they work when applied to everyday situations. These concepts are based on universal life principles and they'll work if you practice them. Just as one and one is two universally, so is the principle of giving and receiving.

One form of giving that was a real challenge for me is tithing. Tithing is giving ten percent of your gross income, that's right gross before taxes, to

128   your church or other source of your spiritual growth.

I had long since graduated from contributing the obligatory one dollar in the collection plate on Sundays to giving sometimes as much as twenty-five dollars. But I had to be convinced that it was in my best interest to tithe. My excuse was always that I just had too many bills to pay, and some months, not even enough money to cover them. I also had heard many ministers give lessons on the subject of tithing. None of them had been able to budge me from my firm position of not tithing. Then one Sunday I heard the minister of my church, Phil Smedstad, give a talk on tithing. This time I really *heard* what he said. It was probably a combination of my finally being ready to make the commitment and actually listening to the different perspective of Phil's talk that moved me to suggest to my wife, Christine, that we begin to tithe.

Phil had suggested that each time the tithe check is written, the tither is nourishing their trust in God as the source of all their good, nourishing their trust in a certain ideal. I suppose also that I was beginning to gain a personal understanding of what God meant to me and, therefore, could accept the belief that God really was the source of all the good in my life.

Have you ever acknowledged God as the source of all your good? It was a concept in giving to which I had never given the slightest consideration. Quite frankly, as many of us do, I had always looked at my place of employment as the source of my financial good and had not given much thought to the other forms of good that came into my life. But I have since learned that money is just one form in which the good in my life comes to me. God, or the universe, is the *source* of all my good, so that even the money I make comes from God.

> The more I thought about and accepted the belief of God as my source, the more it made sense to develop an attitude of giving with respect to that source. Now, for me, that is what giving is all about.

We are nourished mentally by receiving information, but the knowledge only becomes part of us as we use it, just as our physical strength only increases when we use it performing different tasks. This is the way we grow.

> As we stretch our minds beyond our current knowledge by placing ourselves in challenging situations, we nourish the belief that we are greater than we thought we were.

Spiritually, we nourish ourselves by prayer and meditation, by hearing and reading that God is the source of all our good. Reading these principles we may come to believe them, but using them, we come to know them. We see them at work for us, in our lives. When I said in the introduction that I have spent the last fifty years in the laboratory of life, that is what I meant.

Phil suggested that we use the tithing principle by constantly trying to give more away than we receive in goods and services (an impossibility, by the way), by placing our first priority on building our relationship with our source. With each tithe check that's written, we're building a faith and trust in our invisible means of support.

An important point to remember is that by giving money we do not receive money in return. Rather, as we build a richer consciousness, we automatically attract richer circumstances into our lives.

We literally become a magnet for our good, and anyone or anything becomes a possible channel through which we can receive it. Giving and receiving are one in truth.

Affirm that thought with me.

Giving is never restricted to money. We can give in many ways. I was in my forties before I really began to gain insight into personal giving. It was from a book entitled, "On Caring." What stuck with me from that book was the statement, "Give other people what they feel they need, not what you think they need." In an instant, I reviewed my attitude in all my previous and current relationships. I had to learn that giving your partner what he or she wants, not what you want them to have, establishes peace of mind and harmony in a relationship.

Are *you* ready to stop being selfish and start giving? Sometimes you must give in to a situation because your relationship comes first. If you always want to be right, the competition in the relationship will destroy it. You must endeavor to give to the ideal of your relationship; you must give support and cooperation for the relationship to work. When you

132 become responsive to the needs of your mate and start to give, you'll find the support will come naturally and the relationship will start to flow smoothly. In every communication, ask yourself, "Is this communication loving to the other person and to myself? Do I want peace or do I want conflict? If I want conflict, then I will be concerned only about getting or evaluating why I am not getting what I want. If I want peace, I will be concerned only about giving."

The highest form of giving is to give of oneself. You are so much more valuable than any of the material possessions you may have or will ever have. Now for the $64,000 question. What qualities do you wish to increase in your life? Would you like to have more happiness? An easy way to *get* more happiness is to *give* more happiness. Have you noticed that people don't smile at you a lot? When was the last time *you* smiled at someone? Do you think people are just not considerate of your feelings? How considerate are *you* of the feelings of others? We all want more money. How much money are *you* tithing or sharing with charitable causes? Nobody loves you? Who are *you* loving, unconditionally?

> If you are searching for a vehicle to put meaning back into your life, start serving and helping others. Then you'll discover the real meaning of life.

The feelings of satisfaction and gratitude I've received from working with charities and extensively with Literacy Volunteers of America have been more rewarding than anything I've ever done. You too, can experience these feelings once you get in touch with your POWER IN GIVING.

7

THE
POWER IN
IMAGINATION

The real voyage of discovery consists not in exploring new landscapes, but in having new eyes.

What would you like to have more, or less, of in your life? Well, I've got good news. You *can* actually have it by using your imagination. Your imagination is the workshop of the mind. You're on a beach, alone, in the midst of a raging storm. Yet you stand defiant against the winds and rain. Then, the storm ends, the clouds disappear, and the sun emerges to dry and warm your skin. As you lay under a swaying palm tree, a breeze soothes you, and you can almost hear music—sounds of paradise. Down toward the edge of the horizon you see your perfect partner, the soul mate of your dreams.

Have you ever thought what life would be like without imagination? That's something I can't even imagine, because life without imagination is an impossibility. Imagination, that vibrant, exciting dimension of the human mind, is definitely one of our most important human faculties. Your imagination takes thoughts, ideas, plans, and conceptualizes them into a game plan, which begins the journey toward transforming them into material substance.

"But," you say, "That paradise was only in my mind, it doesn't exist, and even if it does, I'm not there." The fact that you *could* picture such a locale means that it *can* exist; if it couldn't, you never could have thought of it. Now you must imagine a way of getting there; use your imagination to transport you to your paradise.

Have you ever thought of your imagination as that place of the soul, or the mind, where thoughts are woven into whole cities, artistic masterpieces, and all manner of creation? Well it is. Doesn't that prove that everything you need lies within you? Doesn't that help you to see how your imagination helps manifest the physical counterpart? Now you can see how powerful imagination is in your life and to your everyday living.

As a child I never imagined I would make it big, but that's the great thing about imagination. You don't need to start at an early age to make it work for you. You can start right now whatever your age and still get results.

Imagination is the power of the mind to form a mental image of something neither real nor present; the ability to confront and shape reality using the creative power of the mind; the formation of mental images, or mental representations of objects or ideas. Whatever you materialize in your life must first be pictured in your mind by your imagination.

For much of my life I associated the use of imagination only with the artistic world. It is true that an artist uses imagination to create art. However, the same is true for anyone, no matter what work they perform. The manager of a supermarket must use imagination in displaying merchandise, motivating employees and dealing with customers.

138   That store manager uses imagination as much as an artist.

I have a friend who works in the kitchen of a prison making salads. He tells me how he constantly uses his imagination to make each salad more spectacular than the previous one.

While making a speech at an IBM regional office in Honolulu I saw an excellent example of the use of imagination in motivating employees. They had reproduced life-size cutouts of movie stars and inserted quotes that related to the theme of the meeting. It proved to be very effective in getting the attention of the employees, while also entertaining and educating them.

Actors and actresses use their imagination to portray characters they have never met or who do not exist. How well they do their job, pretending to be someone different, depends on a lot of factors, one of which is how strongly they use their imagination. An audience watching a good performer will forget that they're watching someone who is imagining he's someone else. That's how real a good dramatic performance can seem. Without imagination, that level of realism would be impossible to achieve. A musician hears notes in his mind, imagines them, before composing a musical score. An author mentally weaves a cast of characters and plots before writing. A business executive thinks in terms of materials, products and services. An artist confronts a blank canvas and from the wellspring of his imagination creates a masterpiece. A mind without imagination is a mind that can't really be functioning. Imagination is an essential part of what we are.

Do you know how many times a day you take your imagination for granted? Probably thousands. Housework may seem a mundane and dreary job, but during the performance of your daily chores you plot out in your mind exactly how you're going to perform each chore and in what order. Often you unconsciously seek ways to express yourself differently. That's because your imagination is present whether you know it or not. The key to making your imagination work for you is to be aware that you can apply it to anything in your life, one project at a time.

One of the factors that motivates me to call upon my imagination is the desire to express myself as a unique individual. Doing things in new ways takes imagination. Once we become locked into one mode of operation we become less reliant on our thinking faculties. When we turn off our imagination we disconnect a section of our minds. We begin a journey down a path of stagnation and mindlessness.

140   I get bored if I have to drive the same streets too often. And let me tell you, in Honolulu, where I live, finding different routes to travel takes a lot of imagination because it's an island. But even there I mix up the streets I use going from place to place.

Imagination is a valuable faculty because it helps you visualize what you want, making it possible for you to act on your desires based on what you've seen in your mind. For instance, when I was a personal manager I wanted to alert producers, directors and casting agents to a client appearing on a TV show. I decided to use a napkin from a famous local deli to send out the message. First, I had visions of people receiving and reading the napkins. Those visions were a product of my imaginative force. I saw the message printed on the napkin in my mind. That was my first draft; I now had something to work with and produce the final product. But then the air date was changed. What was I to do? I didn't have enough time to mail more napkins so I decided to send telegrams to some of the key people. The telegram said, "disregard previous napkin," and gave the new air date. Both the napkin and the telegram were big hits, and we received excellent coverage.

> One of the greatest stimulants for your imagi-
> nation is an emotional involvement with your
> task. You've got to love whatever it is you are
> doing.

There were many evenings when I sat in my living
room, alone, painting mental pictures of what my
cookie business would look like. I constantly visualized my first chocolate chip cookie store in Hollywood, California. I *imagined* all of those pieces
coming together. One of the reasons my plans and
ideas materialized so quickly is that my imagination
was spurred on to an accelerated rate by my own
excitement and love for the project I undertook.
Inspired by Paul Revere's warning, "The British are
coming, the British are coming!" I decided to have
a sign made for the store window announcing, "The
cookies are coming, the cookies are coming!" I saw
the sign on that viewing screen of my mind weeks
before it was displayed in my store window. When I
put the sign up in the store window, it was just as I
had imagined.

I, and others, imagined what the store itself would look like. The atmosphere of an A-frame cottage-style home fit into my concept of what my business should be. The opening celebration, with valet parking, a roving jug band, souvenir posters and balloons, milk, champagne, my friends and their friends all eating free cookies, came directly from the vivid picture I kept in my mind. I created that *brown fever,* which has continued to this day. I created it from an idea. Some of the disbelievers present at my opening cookie festival were saying, "Who would have thought all of this would happen because of a chocolate chip cookie." *I* did! And I did it all with my imagination. I even visualized the mixing bowl and spoon I used when I baked cookies at home, as the center of interest in the Hollywood store. Sure enough, when you walk into Famous Amos on Sunset Boulevard, there they are encased in glass on a pedestal.

My imagination did not stop once I began selling cookies. No, no. I had to continue thinking up new promotional ideas to keep the business going. I remember once being in Tucson, Arizona, on a promotional tour, at a department store located in a shopping mall. I did a takeoff on Air Force One, the president's plane. I arrived in a helicopter I called "Cookie One." I stepped out at the landing site with one cookie nestled on a satin pillow. A motorcade transported us from the landing site to the department store. My youngest son Shawn, who was about nine at the time, sat in the back of a pick-up truck in one of those huge fan-shaped straw chairs and held the precious cookie on the pillow. "What about a band and fanfare?" you might ask. The kazoo, as the official instrument of the cookie, worked wonders. There was a Farrell's Ice Cream Parlor in the shopping center and I went inside and recruited some of their employees to play kazoos in a marching band. The crowd that was gathered supplied all the fanfare I needed. I visualized the event, and then created it. I used talk shows to promote it and get media coverage. I simply took the old concept of an important statesman or dignitary arriving at an event and shaped it to suit my needs. Making something new out of a concept that has been around for a long time is imagination at work. After all, there's really nothing new under the sun.

Visualize, mental picture, realize—these are all words of the imagination; synonyms for "I use my imagination."

144 Have you ever noticed how children use their imaginations much more than adults? They have not yet learned how *not* to use their imaginations. Just the other day my three-year-old daughter, Sarah, was putting water into her little toy pool using her mother's belt for a hose. Throughout the day she is busy creating an interesting and exciting world for herself through her imagination. She is training her mind to do what she wants it to do. It automatically takes that direction without her being aware of it. Sarah's having fun playing. We can call it, "practicing use of imagination," or "playing make-believe." They're the same thing. Now she can create a merry-go-round and ride on one of its many-colored horses. Later, when she's older, she may have to create a science project or term paper. Her imagination will be as important a tool for her then as it is for her now. And if her imagination remains unsuppressed, she will be much more capable then because of the practice she gets now.

It really is possible to take an idea right out of your mind and make it become real. The word "realize" comes from the imaginative process; it means to make real. And what do you make real? What do you realize? That which you've conjured up in your mind with your imagination.

How many times have you been told, "Now,

don't let your imagination run wild." Well, I suggest you disregard that advice and let your imagination run rampant. Release those reins and just let it go. Your imagination is the one thing you have complete control over. No one can even get close to reproducing your imagination. It's probably the faculty that sets you apart from others more than any other. It's all yours. By keeping your imagination in check you reduce the ability to realize your goals. It cripples your mind, limiting your potential to form your own world and reality. Without a game plan, the ability to accomplish even the most simple tasks disappears. No imagination, no game plan. So, you become a weaker individual who must operate within the boundaries of a reality created by someone else. You are being controlled when you do not use your imagination.

Many doctors, and patients too, now believe the mind plays a powerful role in curing or preventing some illnesses. That makes sense, because we know the mind controls the body, not the other way around. Weak minds relinquish control either to their own bodies or to other individuals. But a weak mind, like any weak muscle, can be strengthened. The first step is to let the mind know that it can take control. It's been said we are what we eat. We are also what we think. References to the power of the mind can be found even in the Bible: "As a man thinketh, so is he." Paraphrased: A man makes himself because he thinks.

The expression, "It's all in your mind" usually indicates doubts as to the reality (or believability) of a certain issue. Well, as you gain more understanding and appreciation of your imagination you will start to understand that *everything* begins in your mind. Reality begins in your mind. It's got to begin somewhere, doesn't it? This reminds me of the response my mother gives when she tells people she is the mother of Famous Amos and they don't believe her: "Somebody had to be his mother, why not me?" Imagination has to begin somewhere, why not in the mind?

The use of imagination is nothing more than examining facts, concepts and ideas and then creating new combinations and plans. To bring new life and vitality to an old idea, to an old plan or method, takes imagination. A voyage of discovery can be an exploration of new landscapes. But it can also be the exploration of old landscapes with new eyes. Your imagination then becomes the medium with which you develop your new eyes.

Success stories of others have always bolstered my spirits and inspired me in my own work. I consider them as messages directed to me personally, messages that say, "Wally, success is possible for you, too."

Many people who have become household words have used their imaginations to achieve their dreams. How much do you have in common with them?

William Wrigley, Jr. had to use his imagination to become the kingpin of the chewing gum industry. I think if he could amass a fortune selling chewing gum for five cents a pack, surely there's hope for me and everybody else.

At the age of twenty-six, having just moved to Chicago, Wrigley went into business for himself as a manufacturer's representative. He offered premiums such as chewing gum to motivate his clients. If a client bought baking powder, he would enclose two free sticks of chewing gum with each package. In a short time, customers began writing his office asking if they could just buy the gum. In 1892, Wrigley gave up his other product lines and started selling chewing gum exclusively.

He arranged to have his gum displayed on cash register counters and in display cases in restaurants across the country. Wrigley spent one hundred million dollars on advertising between 1928 and 1931—

148   the largest amount spent on any single product during that time. That took courage and imagination.

William Wrigley proved the value of determination, hard work, perseverance and all the other positive qualities we associate with success. But I feel that above all he showed the value of imagination, because he had to weave a lot of old ideas together to create the many new concepts it took for him to move all that gum. He did, and so can you, because you have the same equipment Wrigley had—a mind that uses imagination.

It's hard to think of baby food without conjuring up the image of the Gerber Baby.

Like many products, Gerber baby food came into existence from a need created within the family that started the company. Dan Gerber's wife, Dorothy, forced him to strain a container of peas to experience what she had to put up with to feed their baby three times a day, seven days a week. Dan decided there had to be an easier way. Since he and his brother, Frank, owned a cannery, they proceeded to find the solution. By the end of 1928 they were ready to go to market with a line of five strained baby foods.

Dan Gerber gave us a glimpse of the way his

imagination worked when he ran his first mail order ad in *Good Housekeeping,* offering six 4.5 ounce cans for a dollar. The hook was that readers had to send in the name and address of their regular grocery store. That ad plus additional ones enabled the Gerbers to establish a distribution network of grocery stores nationally within a three-month period. I'll bet Dan Gerber used his imagination to visualize his customers responding to his promotional ads.

The Gerbers also showed creativity and imagination in other areas. They published books on child rearing and feeding psychology. They bought a fleet of baby-sized Austin cars with horns that played "Rock-A-Bye-Baby," for their salesmen. (As a promoter, I especially love that idea. I had a Volkswagen Rabbit with my picture, a picture of the cookie and the logo on the hood and sides. That car was my only means of transportation during my first years in business.) The Gerbers also were the first baby food producers to advertise on TV.

There's an old axiom: "Find a need and fill it." The Gerbers did just that by letting their imagination run wild with ideas on how to market baby food. And they created an industry in the process. Wasn't that a powerful achievement? Their goal was not to create the baby food industry; they began by

150 trying to make one job a little easier. Their imagination led them on to their subsequent achievements. They probably didn't even realize what they
had done until well after the fact. This story also
illustrates the tremendous benefit received in life
when imagination is put to work one project at a
time

My career as Famous Amos is a similar story. I
took an idea and created a whole new concept that
turned into a new industry—a store selling home-
made-style chocolate chip cookies exclusively. Like
the Gerbers, I had no examples to follow. I had to
imagine everything.

If Wrigley, the Gerbers, and "yours truly" can
make their brainstorms—brainstorms, there's another word that signifies imagination in action—
materialize, so can you. Everything that ever was,
that is, and that ever will be started with an idea.
And the degree to which the idea materializes is
directly related to the amount of imagination applied.

How can you realize more of your potential by
using your imagination? Nothing sticks with you
more than things you practice. You can practice
using your imagination by thinking of a new way to
do something you've done the same way for years.

Begin to take chances. So often we do only those things that are safe or things that have already been done. That's not using your imagination. When we are obsessed with living a safe, secure existence we miss the meaning of life. Security is all a matter of perception. Your mind brought you to the point where you feel secure. Your house, car and job are all material possessions obtained for you by your mind.

> Your sense of security should not rest upon material things, but rather on the force that created them for you—your mind with its imagination.

Life's really an adventure. In order to make it exciting you've got to use your brain. You've got to let your imagination run wild.

How many times have you seen people trying to blend into the crowd forgetting the fact that we're all individuals? They let others create a reality for them to exist in. They're not using their imagination, nor are they using their minds. Our goal is not to be one of the crowd. Even during those times when I was shy and introverted with a poor self-image, there was still something inside me that made me dress outlandishly and carry myself differently, something that made me stand out and get noticed. I realized this was a great quality I had. Find the quality you possess that makes you stand out and put your imagination to work on it.

Often people don't use their imagination because they're afraid of being called silly, stupid or different. Well, you *are* different and you need not be concerned with what people say or think about you. It's only important for you to know that you are a pretty nice person. None of your critics will support you. Remember Terry Cole-Whittaker's book on the subject *What You Think Of Me Is None Of My Business*.

We are all constantly being bombarded by new ideas. Scrutinize those ideas. Begin to be more observant. *STOP BEING A ROBOT.* Begin thinking for yourself.

> When you begin to examine life more by taking the time to see and feel what is happening, your imagination will begin to expand.

Experience is the best teacher, and my experience has taught me that everything you do in life is actually preparing you for something else. Unconsciously, I had been test marketing the cookies for five years when I used them as calling cards during my years as a personal manager. My homemade cookies always opened doors and got rave reviews. Getting rich was not my goal. I was simply doing something well. And I didn't think of opening a chain of stores when I started. I was looking forward to putting my best efforts toward making a quality product in one store, sharing it with people, and having fun. Plain old common sense (which I've discovered is not so common) and a vivid imagination helped me achieve that goal. Obviously there was more to it than I could envision, because look where I am today: selling cookies throughout the United States and Asia, plus doing so many other things as a direct result of the cookie business. Only a small segment of the plan was shown to me, but then with the use of my imagination I was able to visualize the next phase, and then the next, and on and on until here I am, truly Famous Amos.

If you're taking a stab at a business venture, start right where you are knowing that you have been training your whole life for this very moment.

154 Take whatever part of your plan you can see and begin to use your imagination to help you expand it into the big picture it is destined to be. Visualize where the components fit. Move them around in your mind to make them work for you. Take whatever steps necessary to make your ideas materialize. Remember, imagination is the ability to confront and shape reality using the creative power of your own mind.

Imagination in Relationships

How can you use your imagination to improve yourself as an individual in your relationships? Imagine yourself as something and you will begin to become that something. Remember, "as a man thinketh, so is he." You can change any aspect of your existence. Just imagine that change in your mind and it will happen in your life. You've got to ask yourself truthfully, "What am I contributing to this relationship?" Evaluate those areas that need improving. Replay them over and over in your mind. See yourself as a different person in each situation. See yourself giving more love. See yourself as a more patient individual, as a more considerate person. Understand you are not here to change the other person, you are working on improving your contribution to the relationship. By practicing daily imaging and seeing your behavior change you will notice a change in your actions, and ultimately the other person will begin to respond to the new you. It's really important to remember, whatever you see in your mind will materialize in your life. Napoleon Hill in his book, *Think And Grow Rich*, created a formula that says C + B = A: what you Conceive, if you Believe, you will Achieve. The same principles will work for getting a job, a new home or realizing any of your lifetime goals.

Visualize your dream over and over again. The process is just like rehearsing a speech before you deliver it to an audience. You practice at home in front of a mirror; you say it to yourself countless times. Then, when you go before the audience, you're a big hit.

I heard of a situation where a soldier was a prisoner of war in Vietnam for several years. Every day he would imagine himself playing golf and getting a hole in one. When he was finally freed and settled back on U.S. soil, one of the first things he did was play golf. And wouldn't you know it, he made a hole in one even though he hadn't played—physically, that is—for years. Reality starts in your mind.

Just as a sculptor looks at a slab of marble and

156   sees a beautiful work of art inside, you too can use your imagination to create beautiful statues in your life, whether your statues take the form of better health, a job change, a new car, your own business, a more fulfilling relationship, or whatever. You can make it happen through proper use of the power of your imagination. Imagination is a powerful, powerful tool.

On one of my trips to Japan some people were telling me of a Japanese sculptor who carved beautiful statues out of wood. They said he studied the wood he was going to work on for days and sometimes even months before beginning to carve it. They asked him why he studied the wood for so long. He said that he just studied it to get to know it. He would see the object that he was to carve from that piece of wood. When he started carving he simply cut away everything that wasn't the object that he wanted to carve. He used his imagination to see in that piece of wood, the bear, the fish, or whatever it was he wished to carve, then cut away everything that *wasn't* the bear, or everything that *wasn't* the fish. He was letting his imagination run wild, unfettered. Imagination creates all the joy and goodness, all the material things, whatever it is you want in your life. It also creates fear, guilt, and other

things you do *not* want in your life. So, if you first 157
see it in your mind, you can be sure it will be
reproduced in your world. Let your imagination run
wild, and it will act as a funnel for the power in you.

8

THE POWER IN ENTHUSIASM

Age may wrinkle the face, but lack of enthusiasm wrinkles the soul.

o you live your life with an attitude of enthusiasm? When we talk about enthusiasm, we deal once again with attitude. Enthusiasm empowers your life like electricity powers a light bulb. Nothing happens to that bulb until you flip on the switch and release a surge of electricity to illuminate it. In life you become the light bulb and enthusiasm is the switch that turns you on.

160   The word enthusiasm derives from the Greek word *enthousiasmos*, which means inspiration. (I am tempted to change the spelling to enthousi*amos*!) The Greek word *enthous* and *entheos*, meaning "possessed" and "inspired," also became incorporated into what we know today as enthusiasm. It can infect those around you like a contagious disease. You inspire others with your excitement. Charles Fillmore, co-founder of Unity Church, made one of the most descriptive statements ever recorded on enthusiasm and he made it when in his nineties. He said, "I fairly sizzle with zeal and enthusiasm, and I spring forth with a mighty faith to do the things that ought to be done by me." Charles Fillmore knew the importance and value of enthusiasm in life and his attitude toward his daily activities. The concept of enthusiasm contains empowering, activating and invigorating principles. Even the definitions of enthusiasm inspire enthusiasm: "filled with great joy or rapture"; "to be ecstatic or excited"; "possessed with an ardent fondness, eagerness, or zeal." Everytime I read those words I'm actually invigorated and filled with great joy. Already, you must have guessed the importance of enthusiasm in my life. By the end of this chapter, it should be as important to you as it is to me.

People always ask me, "What's your secret, Famous?" I usually respond by saying that I have no secrets or rather the secret is, there is no secret. A disappointing answer to some, because they really want to know how I've done it. Well, reflecting on my life and reviewing some of the many challenges I've faced, one ever-present element comes to mind—my enthusiasm for life. Perhaps that's the "secret ingredient." But enthusiasm is available to everyone, which means it's *not* a secret. Even through disheartening events I've maintained an ability to bounce back, not with bitterness or resentment, but rather with a renewed enthusiasm for life. Those events have taught me that life is never really what it appears to be. It's always more. As far back as I can remember, I responded to adversity with a feeling that said, "Life is good and if I stay positive, I will always move forward, even when I think I'm regressing."

In 1967, a major challenge (actually a major opportunity for growth) occurred while I lived in New York City. I quit my job as an agent at the William Morris Agency where I'd worked for almost seven years. I entered the world of the entrepreneur, going into business for myself as a personal manager. Several months after that, my second wife Shirlee,

162   gave birth to our son, Shawn. A month later, I dropped them off in North Carolina with Shirlee's mother, while I continued on to California to make arrangements for our new life. My life moved along at a pretty fast pace, in definite positive directions. Intense enthusiasm flowed through me as I approached all of my projects. After working for seven years at William Morris, I had grown tired of working with rock-and-roll acts. My request for a transfer to another department had been denied. Deciding to leave William Morris and work for myself as a personal manager would force me to prove myself again. I would work in the same type of career, only with different and new challenges. I would work for myself; the thought made me sizzle with enthusiasm. Shawn's birth, a most positive experience, brought enthusiasm into my personal life. The month that followed, hectic with activity, overflowed with enthusiasm. I had begun a new life in California. During that time, I learned again that enthusiasm helps you enjoy what you do and enables you to perform tirelessly for long periods of time.

Then came the trials. One month after Shirlee and Shawn arrived in Los Angeles, my one and only client, Hugh Masakella, the South African trumpeter, dismissed me as his personal manager. On top of that, he told me that he would not repay the money I had loaned him and his group. My family and I had to vacate the house we had rented because it was in his name. This left me with no job, no place to stay, and no money. If this wasn't enough to make my knees buckle, Shirlee then entered the hospital from total exhaustion. What was I to do? My new life in California seemed to be falling apart.

You may wonder how I could remain enthusiastic. But even back then, in 1967, before I had developed the spiritual understanding I now have, and before I had attended any of the positive thinking self-help programs I now attend or listened to any of the motivational cassettes I listen to now, I maintained an attitude of "this too shall pass." Unity minister Eric Butterworth put it another way. "The Bible says, 'It came to pass. It did not come to stay, it came to pass.' " I took two-month-old Shawn back to North Carolina to stay with his grandmother while I regrouped.

Understandably, Shirlee's entering the hospital did not inspire celebration. Yet, there is a difference between enthusiasm and celebration. I maintained a level of enthusiasm in assuring Shirlee that Shawn would be okay with her mother and that she should just take advantage of this time to rest and recuperate. If ever enthusiasm should be applied, it's when you visit someone who's ill. The best medicine for a patient is distraction. It takes their minds off their illnesses and involves them in some joyful activity.

> A positive mental attitude provides the best environment for the body to heal.

I've visited many hospital wards, both for children and adults, playing my kazoo as enthusiastically as possible, and I could always see the effect in the happy faces. In a children's hospital in Oklahoma City, I made a young child, Mason, smile by playing my kazoo; he hadn't smiled for weeks. This is the attitude of enthusiasm I took to Shirlee when she lay in her hospital bed.

Next, I planned the reorganization of my professional life. I didn't have a filled-with-great-joy enthusiasm; rather, I felt eager, eager to get my business activities moving in new and positive directions. I approached that task with zeal. A lot of my inspiration came from needing to find another source of income. Nothing inspires like the necessity of finding a new source of income. I found new clients to represent, Shirlee recuperated, and once again our lives flowed in positive directions. The preceding events did not signal the end of the world.

Throughout the entire period, I maintained an enthusiastic positive attitude. Every situation we face presents us with the opportunity to view life from an attitude of enthusiasm, if only we choose to do so.

An attitude of enthusiasm in the work place, in helping the ill find relief, if only for a moment, does not know defeat, and cannot comprehend despair.

That's the attitude I took in reorganizing my life.

Enthusiasm Expressed

How many times have you sat through a lecture by a speaker who delivered his speech in a dull, monotone voice where the only benefit you received from the talk was a good sleep? Now, think of all the speakers you've enjoyed, the ones from whom you really learned valuable lessons that enriched your life while entertaining you at the same time. I'll bet you cookies to dollars that the dominant aspect of both their personalities and their lectures was *enthusiasm*. The passion and conviction of their

166   delivery created the fertile atmosphere in which you could absorb their message. The enthusiasm in that atmosphere connects them with you and the rest of the audience. It creates a oneness. I know, because I've experienced moments in lectures I've given when I have felt that oneness with an audience. I felt as if I had literally become the words I spoke. In that type of environment, those words come forth endlessly and without effort. Back in the Love chapter, I pointed out that the key to excelling in your chosen profession is to *become* that profession. Well, I become the words and the thoughts in my lectures and my love and enthusiasm takes me the rest of the way. Why, I'm even the words, sentences and thoughts you are reading now.

A powerful example of enthusiasm is the fundamentalist minister who works himself and his congregation into a fervor. The excitement and enthusiasm become so strong that it overwhelms. Those emotions emanating from one person infect hundreds of others. Think about that church and how it rocks and seethes with the energy created by the enthusiasm of that minister. Does that give you some idea of the incredible power in enthusiasm? Does it give you an idea of the incredible power in you? Enthusiasm does not discriminate, we all can tap into that inexhaustible supply of power.

Our belief system is the major difference between those of us who live a life of enthusiasm and those who live a life comprised of lackluster, plodalong, boring, day-to-day events. Enthusiasm gets choked off in a negative belief system. A negative belief system is nothing more than a collection of values that do not allow you to believe in yourself or in the goodness of life itself. Your beliefs represent your attitude about your existence. If your set of values tells you that you exist by accident, for no definite purpose, and that if any good ever comes your way, it can only be by accident, then you will live exactly that type of life. Enthusiasm will help you escape from that negativity.

If your beliefs tell you that you exist for a definite reason, that you have attracted everything in your life by your attitude and thoughts, then how can you go through life without being enthusiastic? As you go through life (or as Eric Butterworth says, "as you grow through life") you will be doing exactly what you are intended to do in your life. If you're always in the right place at the right time, why not rejoice in everything you do and encounter? Know that each experience is exactly what you should be doing at that instant. That belief in itself will inspire enthusiasm. This concept certainly has given me the confidence to be enthusiastic: the belief that

168   everything I do is right, for my good, as well as the
good of the universe.

I'm sure that Christopher Columbus' belief that
the world was round created the enthusiasm he
projected to Queen Isabella and that convinced her
to finance his expedition. I'll bet Thomas Edison's
belief in the existence of a method to artificially
produce light gave him the enthusiasm to endure ten
thousand trials before his invention of the light bulb.
Enthusiasm must have been the foundation of Henry
Ford's philosophy that says: "Failure is not failure
but the opportunity to begin again . . . more
intelligently." For me, believing that I could open
one store selling chocolate chip cookies created the
enthusiasm, and the desire, which led me to the
achievement of that goal. My enthusiasm in the
project encouraged people to offer their services,
simply for the joy and excitement of the involvement. Enthusiasm becomes the staircase on which
we can all walk up to a higher plane of existence.

Enthusiasm and Belief

> Enthusiasm is the mainspring of the mind,
> which urges one to put knowledge into action.

But you must first believe and have faith in that knowledge otherwise you will never be wholeheartedly involved in any application of the know-how. It can only be considered a feeble attempt to fool yourself, and you will never be able to get others to believe. The late author Napoleon Hill summed it up when he said, "No man can afford to express, through words or acts, that which is not in harmony with his own belief, and if he does so he must pay by the loss of his ability to influence others." Or, more simply, "You cannot afford to suggest to another person, by word of mouth, or by an act of yours, that which you do not believe."

I have had occasion in my life to understand that quote first hand. Advertisers for a certain product once offered me the opportunity to be in a commercial for a considerable fee. However, the product was not one that I used. I had to turn down the job because my integrity would not let me endorse a product I did not use. Even had I agreed to participate in the commercial I could not have done so with any degree of enthusiasm. On the other hand, United Airlines asked me to be in one of their commercials, for less than half of what the other company offered. I accepted because I fly United frequently. While making that commercial, I performed with such enthusiasm that I did some of my best work. My belief and conviction allowed my enthusiasm to flow forth quite naturally.

Through the years, I have developed guidelines to help keep me in a state of enthusiasm. I hope they can do the same for you.

> Never antagonize anything or anyone. Work on leading a life of non-resistance, giving, and service to mankind.

In every situation you encounter ask, "What can I do to make the other person's job easier?" "What can I add to this experience?" I have found that doing this keeps me on friendly terms with everybody I encounter and keeps me in a positive relationship with the entire universe. I cannot be antagonistic and enthusiastic at the same time, so I always choose to be enthusiastic.

"Until tomorrow becomes today, men will be blind to the good fortune hidden in unfortunate acts." That is a quote I keep in mind whenever I'm faced with a challenge and may not be able to see the good involved. I always strive to make the best use of every occasion and situation, even if nothing positive is immediately apparent. Always look at the bright side. By making the best use of every occasion, we attract the best of everything into our lives. Approaching each situation with enthusiasm permits you to see and make the best use of all opportunities.

When I first moved to California in 1967, I faced challenges and wondered why all of those bad, unfortunate events were happening to me. Reflecting on those times now, I can see a lot of the good that I could not see a trace of when I was in the thick of it. Those hardships, which I now consider blessings, forced me to persevere, to be more resourceful. When I lost my one and only client I had to search, not only outside for new talent on which to base my new-found agency, but also to look within for the strength and ability to make my agency work. If I had not been forced to go through those experiences, a tremendous amount of growth would never had taken place. It has taken every experience in my life to create Famous Amos.

Because there is good in every event and situation, I never complain, criticize or condemn. The critical mind *destroys* by labeling something as inadequate and then dismantles it; the learning, searching, believing mind *creates* by seeking to understand, improve upon, grow, and to exist more substantially. A complaint is a mild criticism, and a condemnation is a severe one. Criticisms do not correct. The concept of correction is not built into criticism. The more you complain, the worse events become. Complaining immobilizes by keeping your mind on the problem and so prevents you from seeing or seeking solutions. A condemnation leaves only debris with which to rebuild. How much good can be created from pieces of something that have been condemned?

Enthusiasm and Right Attitude

Let your thoughts and words be constructive, supportive and loving. Those are attributes worthy of enthusiasm. Even if you feel your thoughts unworthy, you will begin to change your attitude about them as you continue to affirm their positiveness with your support and love. And that process works even quicker when you do it with enthusiasm.

Enthusiasm can be applied to everything I've discussed in this book. I talk a lot about living only in the present. When I realize that this moment is all the time there is, I must rejoice *now*; I must be enthusiastic about whatever I'm involved with now. There is no other time. I am alive to experience the blessings of right now. The truth of that statement fills me with enthusiasm and great joy.

I choose to live in a cheerful world. We have a choice in all matters regardless of circumstances. Let cheerfulness be a circumstance you affirm as part of your world. And let your enthusiasm be the proof of your cheery disposition. Being happy is only a decision away and constant enthusiasm is just around the corner from happy.

How much time during the course of a day do you spend being upset over things you can't possibly control? I believe that accepting something that began as a second, third, or even fourth choice, and accepting it with enthusiasm, represents a giant step toward reaching your number one goal. That's exactly what I did at Sak's Fifth Avenue. I took the job as stock clerk with enthusiasm and in less than two years advanced to manager of the supply department. My career at William Morris went the same route. In less than one year I was promoted from a start in the mailroom to full-fledged agent. The steps in between—substitute secretary, permanent secretary, and assistant agent—I mounted with fervor and enthusiasm, yet none of them represented what I had in mind as my optimum career goal. What would have happened to me if I had turned down those first springboard jobs because they weren't my first choice? I would probably still be unemployed, waiting for success to come to me. But no. My

174   present success is a direct result of all the effort I put into my initial efforts. The events of my life have proven to me that whatever comes your way is just another rung in the ladder of your climb to the top. Every experience prepares you for something else. You are always in training. When you accept those experiences with enthusiasm, the climb becomes smoother, more joyful and goes by a whole lot quicker.

There are no secrets to life. Give your best to the world, because you've gotta live here till you leave. You are not a mediocre person, why not be the very best you can? Bring forth the best in everything you touch and everyone you meet, and you in turn will become better and better. Everyone's life will be constantly enriched from without and within; the world will be better because you are here.

Letting your enthusiasm burst forth is like letting your light shine. Don't live your life hiding under a basket. Let your enthusiasm be the beacon that brightens your day and enriches your life, as well as the lives of others.

I would like to close this chapter with an affirmation that will help you raise your level of enthusiasm. Repeat this many times daily (each time with enthusiasm) and I guarantee your life will be filled with joy and ecstasy.

"I AM ALIVE, ALERT, AWAKE AND EN-THUSIASTIC ABOUT LIFE!"

Finally, anything you say or do can be done five times more enthusiastically. So say it one more time—five times more enthusiastically.

"I AM ALIVE, ALERT, AWAKE AND EN-THUSIASTIC ABOUT LIFE!"

As a reminder to myself, I have written the above affirmation on a piece of paper. Directly beneath it I have written a statement given to me by Jim Watt, a junior high school principal in Charlotte, N.C., "I can be five times more enthusiastic." I underlined "five times" five times, tore the sheet of paper in half, then balled both pieces of paper into a little ball. I tied a rubber band around it and now keep it in my pocket at all times just to remind me to be FIVE TIMES MORE ENTHUSIASTIC about everything I do. This can also be a reminder for you to be five times more LOVING, GIVING, etc. Make the same reminder for yourself. We can all be—

FIVE TIMES MORE ALIVE!!!!!

_____

_____

_____

_____

_____

FIVE TIMES MORE ALERT!!!!!

_____

_____

_____

_____

_____

FIVE TIMES MORE ENTHUSIASTIC
ABOUT LIFE!!!!!

_____

_____

_____ _____

_____

_____

9

THE
POWER
IN WORDS

You have to say what you are
if you want to become
what you wish to be.

—Robert Schuller

Just who do you think you are? How many times have you been asked that question? How many times have you been stuck for an answer? I want to help you realize that you are the most powerful human being in your life. Basically, your power comes from two different sources, your mind and your soul. From your mind you get knowledge and imagination: the ability to learn, remember, and apply what you know in countless ways. From your soul you get the motivating desires and attitudes that keep you moving on your chosen

180   path. From your soul comes the reason for being.

The power of your mind is thought. Thought is intangible. And because it is, we must acknowledge that mind power, the power of thought, is primarily expressed through the use of *words*. Words convey thoughts. That makes them one of the most important power tools at our disposal. You might even go so far as to say, the word is everything. We cannot see, hear or smell thought. It is through words that thoughts become accessible to you and me—tangible objects. We can see a written word and hear it spoken. After the thought is absorbed by our senses in the form of the word or series of words, our mind translates them back into thought. Words are the medium for communication.

One great example of this communication is the Bible—the word of God. "In the beginning was the Word and the Word was God." The Bible represents the will of God. It could even be called a physical manifestation of God. God's will is God's thought, which the Bible communicates.

There's a poem in Napoleon Hill's wonderful book called *Laws of Success*, which gives a definition for thought:

> I hold it true that thoughts are things;
> They're endowed with bodies and breath and wings;
> And that we send them forth to fill,

The world with good results or ill
That which we call our secret thought,
Speeds forth to Earth's remotest spot.
Leaving its blessing or its woes.
Like tracks behind it as it goes.
We build our future, thought by thought,
For good or ill, yet know it not,
Yet so the universe was wrought.
Thought is another name for fate,
Choose, then, thy destiny and wait,
For love brings love and hate brings hate.

Indeed, words are powerful tools. Yet, unless we use them carefully and communicate clearly, words are of little value. Many of our difficulties in human relations are caused by improper or inadequate communication. Inadequate communication used to be my specialty, yet only in personal relationships. I never totally committed myself to a relationship, and if my stand on an issue was a little fuzzy, that gave me an easy way out. I never had that problem in business. Professionally, I have always been fully committed to the success of my business ventures, allowing my personal relationships to take second place.

When communication is not clear one of two things occur. Either we do not get our ideas across to other people, or we do not hear what others are saying to us. Usually misunderstandings result.

182   When was the last time you got bent out of shape over words spoken carelessly to you? Did they have a long-lasting, negative effect on your well-being? Remember that experience the next time you are about to use words to reprimand, insult, or criticize others. These experiences act as reminders that nothing positive can ever come from a harmful thought.

   We underestimate how powerful our words and thoughts are not only to the person they are directed to, but to ourselves. It's extremely important to remember that *we* are the first target of our own thoughts and words. And we usually bear their impact long after they have rolled off the back of the person we intended them for. Therefore, when we send out negative thoughts and words they wind up doing far more damage to us personally than they do to anyone else. "Acid can do more harm to the vessel in which it is stored, than the object on which it is poured." Realize the power of your words and thoughts and know that just as you can never retrieve sugar once it has dissolved in the liquid, likewise you can never take back your words once they have left your mouth. Adding words of apology may ease the pain caused by the first words now regretted, but nothing you say or do can take you back in time to *not* say what caused the hurt. The best remedy is to think carefully and not give words to a thought that can cause pain. When you deny that thought long enough it will fade away.

Just as words spoken carelessly can cause pain and misunderstanding, words not spoken at the appropriate time can be equally harmful. I have had years of experience in doing this, also. My relationships, prior to and during the early years of my marriage to Christine, were filled with gaps of silence that begged for compliments, consolations, a word of encouragement, or even the most simple of statements from me: I love you. I can reflect on those times and see how my inability to share and express my feelings had a direct impact on the termination of many of my personal relationships, including two marriages.

I am happy to say, this is no longer the case. Since I realized the importance of words in my life, I have made a conscious effort to be more open and sharing and to communicate accurately. I transmit my thoughts more precisely, and project my power more positively. Because of this, I have added value and meaning to my life and the lives of others. I have also discovered that just as negative thoughts and words affect me immediately, so do positive thoughts and words. The more I can feed that positive food to my subconscious the more abundant

184   my life becomes with joy, love, peace and happiness.

In my travels throughout the United States and other parts of the world, the one thing that has always been constant is *people.* Everywhere I've gone there have been people. From this observation I've concluded that people must be quite important in the grand scheme of things. As a matter of fact, without people there would be nothing; as much importance as we give to computers, they would not exist if a person did not invent them; there would be no banks, no huge cities, nothing, *zippo. People are the bottom line.* So, the ability to communicate with one another must be cultivated and cherished. We are all here together for we cannot exist alone. We are all interconnected. The power in you will be transmitted to others whether you like it or not and whether you're aware of it or not, because that is the order of the universe. So, it's in your best interest to communicate effectively and also to communicate only loving, sincere thoughts. Those thoughts will go out, be received by others, multiplied and returned in kind. You will live a happier, more effective, productive life; non-productive, negative thoughts will simply disappear.

I would like to share with you some words, concepts, and types of thoughts that have helped me create a meaningful and fulfilling life; perhaps they can also help you and those you come into contact with.

Plus Words

Have you ever had an experience where one word had many different meanings? Of course you have. This happens when we use the same word to represent different thoughts. The word "fast," for example, can mean speed used one way. When used another it means abstaining from food. It can relate to your moral standards. If you are in my age group, you have heard about "fast" boys and girls. When I was growing up, I wanted to be friends with the fast girls but never could.

I would like to start with some words we take for granted, yet nevertheless, are words that hold great power. Sometimes we allow that power to be wielded over us, when it is we who should always be in control of the words we use. When you are aware of the power in words you even gain control of those spoken by others to you. You realize it's also your choice in perceiving the words delivered by someone else.

"The world into which we are born is not the world in which we live, nor is it the world in which we will die." That is because everything is in a perpetual state of *change*. *Change* is a concept that

186 challenges us all. We want our lives to remain the same, so we fight against change. Yet the very nature of life is change.

When I wrote my autobiography, *The Famous Amos Story: The Face That Launched A Thousand Chips*, it helped me appreciate and give thanks for all the change I had experienced during my life. Those early-morning writing sessions took me back in time to relive my life. That made me realize that if it had not been for change there would be no Famous Amos. I wouldn't be where I am today, I would be in Talahassee, Florida where I was born. If there was no change I wouldn't have been born, because my birth was change in the life of my mother and father, Ruby and Wallace, Sr. As all living organisms demonstrate, only through change can there be growth; only through change are we able to *become*. The word "become" goes hand in hand with change. How many times have you used the word become? Have you ever thought of it in terms of your personal growth? Becoming the best *you* possible? Sometimes we are so concerned with what we are today that we lose sight of what we are becoming. Remember to live in the present, but realize that the present is in the process of becoming the future. Every day is a time of preparation for the days to come. We are always in training. When we accept this as truth, then even unpleasant experiences can be regarded as lessons in living. I have used knowledge from every experience in my life to sell cookies. So back then, when I was learning what I know now, I was being prepared to become Famous Amos.

Make a decision today to glean a lesson from every experience you have. Tomorrow, you will be a wiser, happier person. Everything has a beginning, but only because of change. Stop resisting. Change gives flow to life and life is change. Get into the flow of life and accept those opportunities for growth that change brings your way. Don't keep looking out the same old window. Accept change and you will find that the new scenery is more beautiful than the old. Accept change in your life and know that this moment is the beginning of the new you, that you are *becoming*, through *change*.

The only way to effectively handle change is through *acceptance*. Don't wish that something had happened differently or at another time, but accept what is at this moment. Acceptance comes with the understanding that you will have another opportunity to correct whatever it is you do not like, but only after you have accepted the experience. Agonizing over past events keeps you stuck in a past filled with pain and unhappiness. Acceptance will

188   lead you straight into *happiness*. Why is *happiness* so elusive to so many people? Do they fail to realize that being happy is just a decision on the reverse side of their decision to be unhappy? Maybe some are like I was for so many years, never knowing that I could have perpetual happiness. We are so locked into the belief of unhappiness as a norm that we start to believe happiness is never attainable. I once heard a talkshow host on national television comment to millions of people that he couldn't believe someone could be happy all the time. He said that if he came across someone who claimed this, he would worry about them. I would be more concerned about someone who was sad all the time. Shouldn't depression be more alarming than happiness?

I believe happiness is our natural state. I believe sadness and depression are learned from others. Have you ever noticed how much easier it is to smile than to frown? Takes less energy too. I also believe we can grow into a state of happiness by being conscious of our words. Stop using negative phrases like, "I don't know the way to happiness," or "I don't know how to be happy." As Dr. Wayne Dyer says, "There is no way to happiness, happiness is the way." Happiness can be defined as a state of being content and joyful. If it *is* a state, a state of mind, and we control our minds and our minds control our reality, then we must be able to choose to be happy. Make a decision today to put some *happy* into your life.

Laughter is the natural expression of a happy state of mind. For as long as I can remember I have loved to laugh. When I was a personal manager, one of my clients, Pat Finley, appeared on the *Mary Tyler Moore Show* from time to time. Whenever I went to a filming of the show, the producers would make sure I sat directly beneath one of the mikes that hung from the ceiling to record audience response. I used to listen for my laughs when I watched the show. One of my favorite pastimes is entering laughing contests. Laughter is infectious. Laugh and the world laughs with you! Laughter even makes friends and disarms enemies. It can rescue you from embarrassing situations, especially if you are laughing at your own embarrassment. (I've had two embarrassing moments with my dentures that continue to give me a good laugh. One happened with Bill Cosby when my upper popped out during conversation with him. Luckily I caught it before it reached the ground. Needless to say, he had a good laugh. The other happened while I was swimming in the ocean one morning. All of a sudden my upper shot out—it's always the upper!—and sank to the bottom before I could retrieve it. Imagine how embarrassed I felt explaining to Christine and later to my dentist,

190   Dr. Courson who had one week to make me another set, what had happened.)

Yes, laughter can truly give you a fresh approach to a challenge and it can help you keep a sense of proportion. Laughter is a sure sign of a healthy disposition. When I laugh, I am aware of how good and enjoyable life can be. When I'm faced with a challenge, laughter helps me to see that every little difficulty is not the end of the world. There's a lot out there that's bigger than my little concern, and laughter helps me to see that.

Laughter is good medicine, too. It makes you breathe deeper, exercise the diaphragm, and it makes the wrinkles that are bound to appear in our faces, pleasant ones. But more importantly, laughter puts you in a positive frame of mind, which is vital to maintaining a healthy body and to healing a sick one. Norman Cousins is a man who contracted a disease diagnosed as having only a one in five hundred chance of being cured and even then never completely. He used laughter instead of painkilling drugs to relax his body, permit him to sleep and begin the healing process, which had been stopped by drugs. Laughter was a major part of his self-made healing regimen, which brought about his complete recovery. For this healing property alone, laughter should be held as very, very precious. It is so much a part of our lives. As someone once said: "The most completely lost of all days is that on which one has not laughed." There are things in this world both good and bad, positive and negative. All of these we have created through the power of our thoughts. Laughter is one of the most positive things. It is something you can take wherever you go, and it can help you in whatever you do. Don't let the sun set on a day that you have not laughed. Find the humor in each day and laugh at it.

What immediately comes to mind when you see the word *nourish*? The main definition is: "to provide with food or other substances necessary for life and growth." A second definition reads: "to foster the development of"; and, also: "promote and sustain."

Usually, we only think of nourishment in terms of the food we eat. But there is another kind of nourishment equally important: the emotional nourishment that we receive from each other.

In this sense, nourishment becomes a word for the soul. Sadie Brown, who owned Collegiate Secretarial School, which I attended when I left the Air Force in 1957, continually nourished the students by reminding them of their enormous potential and encouraging them to always strive for excellence.

192   Later, I was nourished by Ernie Riccio at Saks Fifth Avenue. Ernie would share his business publications with me and he advised me to learn as much as I could about the supply department where we worked at Saks. He made it a point to explain things to me, and always patiently. His nourishment enabled me to ultimately become manager of the supply department.

When I joined the William Morris Agency, I was nourished by Howard Hausman, a senior executive. I was Howard's secretary and he made it a point to have me sit in on meetings or listen in on phone calls so I could be aware of the many situations he was involved in. He also made it a point of taking me to screenings of films, plays, and other activities. Howard's nourishment went a long way in building my self-esteem and self-confidence—two other very important words.

The nourishment I received in these cases was encouragement. I was always told that I could do it, that I had the ability to do it if I wanted to. Whatever *it* happened to be. Encouragement goes a long way in increasing the power of an individual to accomplish, to exist in a wholesome manner. Encouragement, compliment, appreciate and gratitude are all nourishing words made up of good, positive thoughts that feed the soul.

The emotional nourishment I received from Sadie Brown, Ernie Riccio, Howard Hausman and countless others throughout my life played a very important part in helping me to shape my life. Nourishment for the soul increases the intensity of your power. We all need to receive it. And, equally important, we all need to give it to others. Nourishing benefits the nourisher as well as the nourishee. By helping someone to grow and to exist more completely, you help yourself by affirming your purpose here in this world. And that purpose is to serve one another. Besides, who knows when that someone will come back around to help you?

How many times have you missed achieving your most cherished goal? How strong was your *desire?* Desire is another one of those super important words of the soul. If you don't have it, your chances of doing anything of importance are very slim. The dictionary defines "desire" as a "strong wish," and a wish is defined as a "turning of the mind toward doing." These definitions convey how having an earnest desire gives you the endurance to accomplish something that otherwise might not get done. The pursuit of an honorable desire provides a reason for existence in a person's life. A desire to *become* gives you a goal to strive for. Napoleon Hill refers to that striving as a "Burning Desire." I had that burning desire when I was forming Famous Amos. Desire applied to an idea is the same as pouring fuel into a powerful engine to keep it running.

I honestly feel it is impossible to fail when you have that "Burning Desire" to succeed. Examine the lives of great achievers and I'll bet the thing they all have in common is a "Burning Desire." Listen to the voice of desire within you. Interpret it positively. Then fasten your seatbelts and soar in the direction of its fulfillment. All of life's goodness awaits you if your *desire* is strong enough.

Do you know the formula for *friendship*? To gain a friend, be a friend. Friendship is one of the great reciprocal acts of life. Perhaps your closest friend is your spouse. The strongest marriages are those formed on the foundation of friendship. It has taken me a long time and a lot of work to realize and accept that simple truth.

A poem entitled, "This is Friendship," by Mary Carolyn Davies, gives the most succinct interpretation of friendship I've ever read:

> I love you, not only for what you are,
> But for what I am with you.
> I love you not only for what you have made of yourself,
> But for what you are making of me.
> I love you for the part of me that you bring out.

I love you for putting your hand into my heaped-up heart

And passing over all the frivolous and weak things that you cannot help seeing there,

And drawing out into the light all the beautiful, radiant things

That no one else has looked quite far enough to find.

I love you for ignoring the possibilities of the fool in me

And adding to the music in me by worshipful listening.

I love you because you are helping me to make of the lumber of my life,

Not a tavern, but a temple,

And of the words of my days,   (

Not a reproach, But a song.

I love you because you have done more than any creed could have done to make me happy.

You have done it without a touch, without a word without a sign.

You have done it by being yourself.

After all, perhaps this is what being a friend means.

How many friends like this do you have? How often are you a friend like this to others? Maybe it will help if you remember, "a stranger is just a friend you haven't met before."

Minus Words

Words embody both negative and positive concepts, packages of thought. Let's look at some of the words which I feel create negative thoughts, words you should want to erase from the blackboard of your mind. These negatives will only choke off your stream of power and eventually lead to an unwholesome, unfulfilled, and unproductive existence.

How much *regret* do you have over things done or said in the past? "Regret" says that you wish you had not done or said something in your past. "Regret" is a word we should let go because it mires us in the past. It is impossible to leave the present and return to the past to make adjustments in our lives. Release the past and enjoy this precious moment that has been given to you right now.

Did you ever consider that *if,* a small word that packs a big punch, has probably been one of your biggest obstacles? While *regret* is preoccupied with the past, *if* is preoccupied with both the past and the future. With the past, "if" is just like "regret": "*if* only I had . . ." Why even bother? You didn't, so make what adjustments you need to make now, forget it, and move on. Just make sure you take advantage of the opportunity the next time around. The future hasn't happened yet, so don't worry about it. Sure, you make plans for the future, but after you have formalized the plans the best way to have them materialize is to give as much positive energy as you can to them today. And after that, don't worry.

Worry, by the way, is definitely another word to erase. It only gives you wrinkles and ulcers. Think back on all the times you worried and you will very clearly see that in no way did it help you through the difficulty; rather, worry immobilized you and helped bring to pass whatever it was you were worrying about.

The literal translation for worry is, "to strangle." How many good ideas have you strangled to death?

Do yourself a favor, just for today? Don't use any of these words in any of your conversations and witness how it transforms your communication, and then begins to transform your thoughts and, ultimately your life.

I would join you *but* I *cannot.* "But" and "cannot" are words of contradiction and limitation. The little three letter word, *but,* carries with it a whole way of life for many people. What "but" does is to deny or contradict whatever you say. "But" is a word of deception that lets you make statements, often negative, without appearing to have said anything negative at all. How many times have you said something like, "I like him but he dresses strangely."

198   What you actually mean is that you don't like him *because* you think he dresses strangely. Another example: "I really want to be involved, but I don't know if I can." That translates to: "I really do not want to be involved." Eliminating "but" from your vocabulary will make your communications more direct and more truthful.

Cannot embodies a concept of limitation. When we think in terms of our limits we will always remain beneath them. I did not think in terms of *not* opening a store selling chocolate chip cookies. If I did, Famous Amos would never have been born. I would have said: "I can't open a store selling just cookies; I can't open another commissary; I can't sell cookies in Japan, it's so far away." And that is exactly what would have happened. I wouldn't have done anything because I said that I couldn't. Do not define yourself in terms of what you think you *can't* achieve. Develop your life around what you want and who you are and what you *can* achieve, now. Remember, the person who says, "I can" and the person who says, "I can't" are both right. Decide today to be an "I can" person.

Because our thoughts are so powerful we must train them to work for us. I don't think in terms of *problems* because the word *problem* carries with it a whole philosophy of defeat. We have come to believe there must always be problems. And our problems usually get the best of us. I think in terms of *challenges*, because a challenge is something you can meet and surmount. I also view challenges as opportunities for growth.

I don't *try* to do anything. *Try* is another word of limitation. Are you one of the many who believe that giving a thirty percent effort to accomplish a task counts more than whether or not that task gets done? If you are, then the statement "I tried" is good enough. If getting a job done is your goal then if you try and don't get it done, the goal remains unaccomplished, even though you've tried. The *Star Wars* philosopher Yoda put it very well when he said: "Do or do not, there is no try."

These are some of the words that have added value to my life, and those that I did not care to have influencing my power. I hope they demonstrate my idea of the importance of words and how there is no such thing as casual conversation. You project your energy through everything you say and do, and if you're not careful, negative thoughts will slip out and nothing good will ever come from it. Give more importance to your words. Realize their tremendous power, and use only those words that support, encourage, and are truthful, happy and joyful. Use positive words and watch your power soar.

10

THE
POWER
IN FAITH

For every web begun,
God sends the thread

How strong is your faith? That is the question a minister friend, Herb Goeas, asked repeatedly during a sermon he delivered one Sunday morning. It is a question I have asked myself repeatedly ever since. Oftentimes, the reply I receive tells me I have a lot of work to do on strengthening my faith. When I review my life and see the road I've travelled, it is evident that I was demonstrating faith, even though I did not have a full understanding of what faith was. There are times when I still do not have a full understanding of what faith is.

Faith played an important role in my life long before the Famous Amos Chocolate Chip Cookie made its debut in Hollywood, March 9, 1975. It was faith in myself that helped me overcome numerous obstacles that set the stage for my becoming Famous Amos.

I entered the world, July 1, 1936, the only child of an economically poor family, at the height of racial segregation, in a small wooden frame house near the railroad tracks, in Tallahassee, Florida. When I was twelve, my mother and father divorced and I moved to New York City to live with my Aunt Della, Uncle Fred and their son Joe. With six months remaining before graduation from Food Trades Vocational High School, I decided I no longer wanted to be a cook so I quit high school and joined the Air Force. As I look back on those experiences in my life I can see how faith played an important part in my development. What else could have possibly helped me make each transition that proved to be so vital to my growth? At that stage in my life, however, it was not a spiritual faith I had, but a faith in the goodness of life, people and myself. I've always had an underlying belief that things would work out.

As I read the definition of faith, it occurred to me that my success as Famous Amos conforms to one of the definitions of faith, defined as, "confidence in the truth and value of a person or idea." I know I fully trusted myself, as the person, and the soundness of the idea to open a store selling only chocolate chip cookies.

Another definition says, "faith is a belief that doesn't rest on logical proof or material evidence." That tells me that faith is determined by neither the intellect nor the past. It is a moment to moment happening, which also must mean that it can be renewed from moment to moment.

How much thought have you truly given to faith? It is something we use every second of our lives and yet it is the one aspect that we take for granted. When you take a truthful look you will find that your every action exercises some degree of faith. We are constantly venturing into the unknown, to a time and space we have never experienced before. How do we know our plans will materialize? The answer is, we don't. We just have *faith* that if we plan and perform to the best of our ability, everything will happen as we planned it.

The single most significant experience to help strengthen my faith was the pregnancy of my wife, Christine. It was while she carried our daughter Sarah, and witnessing Sarah's birth. That one act had a profound effect on my life and most definitely solidified my faith in God.

Considering that we start life as something so small you need a microscope to see it and within that drop is the design for our total being. Doesn't that thought give you hope that there must be some order in the universe? If it doesn't, then take the thought process one step further and think about how that drop evolved over a nine-month period into YOU, a one-of-a-kind collector's item. During that nine-month period we are loved, nurtured and, without any help from us, God assembles us with all parts functioning and in their perfect place. Also, during those nine months, we display the strongest show of faith by not interfering. I often think that if we had our adult intellect we would be interrupting at every stage of the process, putting in our two cents on where we think the various parts should go. We'd probably have our eyes on the front of our big toes so we could see where we are going.

Do you think God would spend so much time

creating a masterpiece and then abandon it? I don't think so. Being present at Sarah's birth plus gleaning the insight from Christine's pregnancy gave me the faith to know that the same Force—Love or God— that created me is still present in my life to help bring into my world whatever it is I desire. When you have faith in a higher power, you know everything will be provided for you. Is a spider concerned about whether he will have enough thread to complete a web? Is the apple tree concerned whether it will have a full tree of apples? Obviously, the answer is no. The spider and the apple tree just go about the business of being, having faith that their needs, however great or small, will be met abundantly. One way to increase our faith is to live life *being* instead of *doing*.

Have you ever considered that maybe God is not finished making you yet? Maybe our whole life is just an evolutionary process. Isn't that what happens with so much of nature? And aren't we a part of nature? That seems to be the lesson that "Professor" Sarah is teaching me. When she was twelve months old, we were playing on the living room floor and all of a sudden, she pushed herself up, using my head as a balancer, and took her first three steps. What a demonstration of faith that was. How did she know it was time to take those first steps and who taught her how? I have watched her step out on faith many times. Each time it has caused me to reexamine my faith and maybe venture a little further than I ordinarily would have.

I believe that Sarah has been my most influential teacher of faith. From birth she has had the utmost faith and she doesn't have a clue as to what it means. Still, her every need has been met.

Faith in Supply

For her first two-and-a-half years of life, Christine breast-fed Sarah every day. During the early days of her life she was fed as much as twelve times within a twenty-four hour period. Both Christine and Sarah had faith that the milk being consumed would be replenished. (A great lesson in giving and receiving.) Also, Sarah's skin is smooth and without a single blemish and that feat has been accomplished without the use of any of the many skin care products advertised for babies. Demonstrating the faith of a baby, Sarah knew that God would protect and nourish the skin he gave her. She can see, hear, feel, smell and taste, She thinks, talks, walks; she is a wonderful child of God! AND SO ARE YOU!

You entered the world in the same manner as Sarah, and like her you're entitled to all of God's life and entitled to it in abundance. You were given all the tools at birth and can start right where you are. All you need do is to have faith in your inner guidance, the God in you, right where you are this moment.

Do you believe having faith implies a risk? If so, perhaps you might want to check your perspective. Or, as they tell Sarah in nursery school, "put your thinking cap on." Our every action is at risk because there are really no guarantees. Nobody knows.

I'd like to share a writing that talks about risk and has helped to strengthen my faith. The author is anonymous. (Isn't it amazing how many great pieces are written by Anonymous?!)

"Your strongest values can stand the test of challenge. You will risk a lot to act on things that are most important to you. If someone you love were in danger of drowning, you might risk your life to save him. Or if you believe strongly in justice, you might risk ridicule to stand up for someone who is being treated unfairly. All risks—reaching out, testing yourself, trying new things, accepting challenges—involve putting your values on the line. Sometimes the greatest risk may not be climbing the sheer rock face of a steep mountain. It may be more risky to tell someone you care about that you're

208   lonely or to say, 'I'm sorry.' There are many kinds of
      risks in life, emotional, intellectual, and physical.
      The important ones are those that help you grow
      and express your values."

To laugh
    is to risk appearing the fool.
To weep
    is to risk appearing sentimental.
To reach out for another
    is to risk involvement.
To expose feelings
    is to risk exposing your true self.
To place your ideas, your dreams, before the crowd
    is to risk loss.
To love
    is to risk not being loved in return.
To live
    is to risk dying.
To hope
    is to risk despair.
To go forward in
    the face of overwhelming odds is to risk failure.
But risk we must.
Because the greatest hazard in life
    is to risk nothing.
The person who risks nothing does nothing, has
    nothing, is nothing.
He may avoid suffering and sorrow, but he can't learn,
    feel change, grow or love.
Chained by his certitudes, he is a slave.

He has forfeited his freedom.
Only a person who risks is free.

A strong faith puts the odds in your favor thereby helping you eliminate the risk factor.

Faith in Your God

Many people have the misconception that they are controlled by outside forces. They feel that someone else holds the power over their emotions—that they need another mate or someone other than themselves to make their life complete. When you are able to view life from a spiritual perspective you see that God is the creator, supporting you all through life. Everything begins inside of you. Since you create everything in your world, whether consciously or subconsciously, life truly is an inside job!

There have been many examples throughout history of lives lived in faith. Surely at the top of the list is Jesus Christ, who was a great teacher because he taught from his own experiences and through demonstrations. He encouraged us to do the same and even greater things than he did.

Thomas Edison had faith when he set out to find the right filament for the light bulb. It took him ten thousand attempts. It had to be his faith in knowing the answer would be found if he continued to persevere.

Surely it was faith that caused Charles Lindbergh to make his historic solo flight in the Spirit of St. Louis, a single engine plane, from New York to Paris.

It was faith that enabled Ghandi to stand up against Britain and change the course of history by gaining India's independence. It was faith that helped Martin Luther King, Jr. open American society to people of all races, creed, and color.

It was faith that made Noah hear God's warnings about things in the future he could not see or understand. It was faith that made Abraham obey when God called him to go out to a country which God had promised him. He left his own country without knowing where he was going.

I *know* it was faith that made it possible for a guy named Wally Amos, with no retail experience whatsoever, to start a business based on a single product, a chocolate chip cookie, and it was faith again that kept me going when I lost two investors just ten days before the opening of my first store in 1975. They had been out of town and when I finally did reach them they advised me they had changed their minds and decided not to invest. Without missing a beat, I thanked them, went into my office and began leafing through my address book in search of another name I felt I could get $10,000 from. I moved immediately to another game plan. I remained positive and kept a strong faith in myself and my idea.

That idea was the fact that I had been baking cookies at home for five years and sharing them with friends, whose comments were always the same, "Wally, these are great cookies, you should sell them." So in October of 1974 I decided to do just that. By adding a pinch of common sense, a dash of belief in myself and my idea, and a giant helping of faith, I began to gather the elements I thought necessary to open a store selling chocolate chip cookies.

I held firmly to my goal. At no time did I allow the negative thought of not succeeding to enter my mind. Almost five months from the day I made the decision and commitment to open my store, I opened the doors for business to the first store in the world to sell only chocolate chip cookies.

Faith Plus Action

Mine is just one of countless success stories throughout time that tell us that an idea mixed with a portion of faith—even if it's only as big as a

212 mustard seed—will produce positive results. However, faith without action is useless.

Where do ideas come from? That's a question I would think about every time someone would ask me, "Where did you get the idea to open a store selling chocolate chip cookies?" Where did I get the idea? Did I get it from B. J. Gilmore, who said to me, "Wally, we should open a store selling chocolate chip cookies." B. J. actually was the person to push me through that invisible barrier that separates us from *maybe* to *I will.* But, even if the idea came from B. J., where did *she* get the idea? It seems to me that all ideas are inspired by a higher force, God, or whatever you choose to call your creator. I believe that ideas are constantly being channelled through us. We are nothing more than a cylinder through which millions of ideas flow daily.

I've heard it likened to the frequencies on a radio dial. If you want to get 105-FM on your dial, you must tune your radio to 105 on your FM dial. Now when you decide to change to another station, 105 is still broadcasting, you just can't hear it because you are now listening to another frequency.

I believe The Universe has many ideas circulating throughout it. When you get in tune with The Universe—by having faith and allowing The Higher Source or Power to work through you—you become

a fine-tuned channel for those ideas to flow through.
Just because you do not hear the ideas does not mean
they are not there. It just means you have tuned to
another frequency.

I also believe with each idea comes a how-to
kit with detailed instructions, just as instructions are
packed with all those wonderful toys you buy and
assemble for your child at Christmastime. Whether
or not we see the instructions depends on our belief
system.

What stops us is believing that someone else
will supply the action and the know-how. We sometimes believe that everyone, except us, has the
know-how and can perform. Please know from this
moment on that you are an idea expressed. At birth
you were imprinted with a set of instructions and
given the tools to enable you to overcome any
challenge and to complete any task that you could
possibly think of. You need only to have faith and
believe in YOU. Have faith in the God in you.
Listen to that still, small voice called "instinct" or
"intuition" that not only tells you *when* to act but
how to act as well. Just begin to follow the instructions received. Remember the spider. He does not
wait. He begins to spin his web knowing the thread
will appear.

Sarah entered the world stark naked. Not one

214   stitch of clothing. No designer jeans. No jewelry, no material possessions at all. She had no computer software; however, she did have the most powerful computer ever created, her brain. She had the computer that created the computer. It's the only piece of equipment she will ever need to create any material possession she will ever desire. The software is built into the system (or hardware as it were) and God is the programmer.

Faith Put to the Test

So, here's another $64,000 question. How strong is your faith? Is it strong enough for you to leave the job that's no longer fulfilling that you've been threatening to leave for years, knowing a better job is heading toward you? I remember quitting my $85.00-a-week supply department manager's job at Saks Fifth Avenue in 1961 without any idea of where my next paycheck would come from. My wife and I had a two-year-old son and she was pregnant with our second child. I just knew I could get a job as good as, if not better than, the one I had at Saks. I landed a position at the William Morris Agency, which offered the most exciting career opportunity of my life. It happened because I had faith that life had more to offer than Saks Fifth Avenue.

I held a confident belief in the truth, value, and trustworthiness of Wally Amos. As I've said, my experiences have taught me that life is never really what it appears to be, it is always more.

How strong is your faith? Are you ready to start believing in *you* today? Do you have faith that the same God that created you is still with you? He has to be, because he is not finished making you yet. Are you ready to begin believing that you're worthy and totally capable of living a fulfilled life today; to know that there's abundance to satisfy your every need; to have the faith that you can have the perfect relationship?

How strong is your faith? Is it strong enough to push aside all negative thoughts that enter your mind and replace them with positive thoughts that help you believe in the goodness of life and the support of your creator? Are you ready to believe that you really are a channel through which fantastic ideas flow? Please believe it because it's true.

On a recent trip I gained a new insight into faith. I awoke on a Saturday morning in San Diego where I was scheduled to give a speech at noon, take a short flight after the speech to Los Angeles and

216 deliver another speech that evening at 5 p.m. A routine day, except for the fact that I had a severe case of laryngitis when I woke up. I could barely whisper.

Since I was writing this chapter on faith during that period I thought it would be a good opportunity to put my faith to the test. I followed my guidance and made tea with lemon, sucked on throat lozenges and even took advice offered by a friend. I did all this with a knowing that I would definitely be able to make my speeches without any difficulty.

During this experience I also received what I believe to be a deeper meaning of faith. It occurred to me that faith also means trusting a higher plan than your own. It means trusting and accepting the final answer even though it might be different from one you expected. Having faith in a divine plan that your limited human vision is not able to see. Perhaps God thought I would be more effective as a speaker that day with laryngitis. All I know is I did give two very effective talks that touched my audiences in a meaningful way.

How many times have you said, "Seeing is believing"? I don't mean to burst your bubble, but "Seeing is *not* always believing." I'm sure there are many times you can recall seeing the results from the force of the wind, but never once did you actually see the wind. Just because you cannot see the good that is formulating in your life does not mean it's not happening. It might just require your letting go of your negative belief system and replacing it with faith in the positive things of life. That's exactly what happened to me in opening Famous Amos. In letting go of my desires for material things and focusing only on the positive, I opened a cookie store with the goal of only making a living. In the process I acquired more material possessions than I ever thought possible. The concept of faith was at work even though I was not aware of it. If we can become aware of the power in faith and apply it daily in our lives, it stands to reason the quality and value of our lives will increase.

The next time the ugly head of fear knocks on your door, let faith open the door and you'll find there's no one there.

Dear Friend,

Thank you! I sincerely hope in reading this book you have gotten more in touch with The Power In You.

Chose to have a joyous and wonderful life.

Aloha,

Wally

Wally